BETWEEN STILL WATERS AND SWEETGRASS

# Between Still Waters

# and Sweetgrass

*Angelica Arie*

XULON PRESS ELITE

Xulon Press Elite
2301 Lucien Way #415
Maitland, FL 32751
407.339.4217
www.xulonpress.com

© 2021 by Angelica Arie

All rights reserved solely by the author. The author guarantees all contents are original and do not infringe upon the legal rights of any other person or work. No part of this book may be reproduced in any form without the permission of the author. The views expressed in this book are not necessarily those of the publisher.

Printed in the United States of America.

Paperback ISBN-13: 978-1-6628-0578-3
eBook ISBN-13: 978-1-6628-0579-0

For my family: The Greatest Love Story Ever Told

# Table of Contents

| | | |
|---|---|---|
| **Chapter 1** | What God Has Joined Together—<br>Let No Cow Separate . . . . . . . . . . . . . . . . . . . . . . . 1 | |
| **Chapter 2** | The Branding . . . . . . . . . . . . . . . . . . . . . . . . . 12 | |
| **Chapter 3** | There's a Cow in My Room! . . . . . . . . . . . . . . . .21 | |
| **Chapter 4** | Everyone Has a Goliath. . . . . . . . . . . . . . . . . . 29 | |
| **Chapter 5** | Camo Girl . . . . . . . . . . . . . . . . . . . . . . . . . . . 36 | |
| **Chapter 6** | The Upside-Down Trail . . . . . . . . . . . . . . . . . 40 | |
| **Chapter 7** | To Everything There Is a Season . . . . . . . . . . . 69 | |
| **Chapter 8** | Our Faith Is Tried by the Fires of Affliction . . . 87 | |
| **Chapter 9** | Beauty for Ashes . . . . . . . . . . . . . . . . . . . . . . 100 | |
| **Chapter 10** | The Great Montana Sheep Drive . . . . . . . . . . 122 | |
| **Chapter 11** | Keep On Truckin' . . . . . . . . . . . . . . . . . . . . . 145 | |
| **Chapter 12** | A Christmas Miracle? . . . . . . . . . . . . . . . . . . .191 | |

Sam and Kat. . . . . . . . . . . . . . . . . . . . . . . . . . . . . . . 219

CHAPTER 1

# What God Has Joined Together— Let No Cow Separate

Kasiandra Ann Patterson woke to the sound of her name being hurled up the staircase like a blasphemy. It was the "dad voice." This was the voice that implied there would be no second calling, failure is not an option, and there would be no excuses accepted, not even if you were to present your own death certificate, signed and stamped. It was time to get up and get going, and that was the size of it.

She was certain that her two older brothers' names had been cast as well, in their usual order from oldest to youngest—Brett, Axel, and Kasi-Ann, as the family had taken to calling her since she was a baby, followed by the "Let's Go" that meant breakfast is ready, and you're already late.

Samuel Patterson was an impressive and intimidating entity. The seasoned Montana cattle rancher stood a head taller than most men with broad shoulders and an aura of "just try me" that emanated about three feet from him in every direction. His voice was booming and powerful, but underneath all the muscle lay the most tender of hearts. At least that's what Kathryn Patterson would say of her husband and how the cowboy had won her heart.

Kat had become his sweetheart in grade school after Sam had come to her rescue on the playground, knocking a bully down at the monkey bars for pestering her. He had gone to the principal's office defending her honor, and they were the best of friends from that day on. After high school, and the untimely death of his parents, Sam took over the family ranch while Kat went off to nursing school. The wedding waited only a day after graduation.

Kasi-Ann was on the edge of her bed pulling on socks as the smell of sizzling bacon drifted lazily up the two-story ranch house stairs and bid her nose good morning. She loved it when her dad cooked breakfast. Not that her mother was any slouch in the kitchen, but there were just some things that Sam flat-out bested her at, and breakfast, on the whole, was one of them. The five-feet-six-inches fiery redhead would roll her eyes each time everyone went on and on about Dad's amazing biscuits and gravy. Eye rolling could potentially begin when Sam would put "Whack Biscuits" on the grocery list in preparation for making his renowned breakfast. These were the kind that came refrigerated in tubes that he whacked on the countertop, causing them to spring open, obviously exacting his strength over them. Kat chided that he whacked them because the suspense of pulling the label until it popped, as instructed, was too much for him, and the single whack method saved his *cowboy pride*.

Kasi-Ann was the first to respond to the flapjack feast the "Dad Voice" had beckoned everyone to this morning. Kat was still pulling up the comforter on their giant log-framed bed when Kasi-Ann landed in the middle of it, surprising her with a homemade Mother's Day card. It was her favorite thing in the world—a homemade treasure someone had taken the time and care to prepare. She sat down on the bed to carefully open and read what could be a potential glitter bomb knowing Kasi-Ann's love of glue and sparkly things. A simple "Mom, You're The Best Mom Ever, And I Love You" leapt from the colorful page. Kat hugged Kasi-Ann, telling her it was her most beautiful card yet and that she was the luckiest mom in the world to have such a kind, and thoughtful daughter.

The warm embrace ended with an unsuspecting tickle attack on Kat's part while they headed off to the kitchen. Kasi-Ann squealed and ran off in search of one of Sam's famous platter-sized pancakes. She quickly spotted hers already plated and set aside. It had two smaller pancakes cooked into the top to make it look like Mickey Mouse as he had done for her since she was old enough for solid food.

"Thanks, Dad," she shouted as she grabbed her plate and without slowing down, made her way to the sprawling log table. She had to duck and weave to dodge the now-assembling brothers who were always ready to teasingly attempt a hijack of whatever she happened to have in her hands. If it was especially appealing, the feigned hijack could become the genuine article, or at least a pleading for a shared portion. When everyone had arrived at the table, Kat said the blessing, and breakfast came and went with the outlining of the events for the branding, and what each person's job would entail. The boys would trade off roping and wrestling, Kat would be in charge of vaccines, Sam would take care of branding and banding and Kasi-Ann would see every part of the action, depending on whom she was with at the time. Brett would likely grab her and continue teaching her to wrestle when he took a break from roping, lending his strength to make her feel more confident. She would also likely be the gopher much of the day, being sent hither and yon to fetch both things and people to the places they were needed.

With breakfast cleared away, it was barely six o'clock this crisp, May morning. Cattle that had been recently rounded up and trailed to the ranch corrals were bawling out their displeasure in being removed from the soft new green grass and placed in the muddy slop yesterday's spring rain shower had provided. The wooden corrals wore years' worth of Montana weather wear. The gate hinges creaked and groaned a familiar tune as the family traversed through the muck to begin the task of sorting. Later the ranch would be crawling with friends, family, and neighbors who had come to help with the branding, but this morning, it was just family—no witnesses.

Therefore, this spring day, for the family, also held the possibility of a DIVORCE. It was both a family and community joke that cattle sorting could be one of the largest tests upon a married couple, and the Patterson pair was no exception. While it could be trying at times, it was thankfully, just a joke.

Sam Patterson would admit to anyone that he could become somewhat overzealous in his instruction and prone to episodes of spouting unsolicited and colorful critique when it came to sorting cattle. In this case, they would be sorting off the calves that needed to be branded from their mothers, calves going into one pen while mothers go into another, out of the way. The Patterson children could easily have been born in one of their many barns and cut their teeth on baling twine, but it was not contested that Sam's knowledge and experience with stock far outweighed that of everyone else combined. It was also not contested that his "delivery" in the delegation of orders could lack a certain measure of sophistication you might assume any good leader would possess.

On occasion when his body language joined the crusade, the fit could potentially be mistaken by onlookers for a demon possession complete with an admirable attempt at self-exorcism and speaking in tongues. On the days that he continued to use expressions of the English language, Kasi-Ann would find either Brett or Axel suddenly behind her with both hands clapped firmly over her ears until the dust had settled, the slang had subsided, and the work could again resume. The three siblings were well versed in their father's methods and took most things in their stride; however, Kat was another business altogether.

Kat had a gentle, kind and forgiving countenance. Her springy red curls were as playful as her personality, and everyone she saw was met by a warm smile and sparkling green eyes. But a pushover she was not. She would be the calm voice of reason during the Patterson's personal rainstorms until the first lightning bolt was thrown, and then you could almost *see* the thunder. She could blister and burn you down at a whisper as she was not one to reduce herself to common yelling. When she was angry beyond words, a swift retreat toward the shop or the stalls of an obliging barn was highly recommended.

Kat spent the three minute walk from the house to the corrals, praying fervently that this endeavor could be swift and successful, and that any temptation to throttle Sam right there in the mud before its completion could be overcome. As she rationalized that this would be easier due to the ease in identifying the difference between the calf and mother, she couldn't help but mentally drift back to the last corral encounter ...

*****

The last sorting event was in mid-February. Calving was just getting underway and a large mob of the mothers-to-be were waiting in the corral in preparation to sort off the heavies—the cows that would calve soon. They could then be moved into a makeshift maternity-ward barn where the newborn calves had the luxury of a straw-strewn floor instead of a harsh Montana snowbank to greet them.

But first, the Pattersons had to get into close company with chaos and several dozen mammoth, all look-alike, black mother cows, trying to decide which ones looked the part for the express lane, and which ones would be content to wait a week. Inside the corral, it was a mix of family reunion and Sunday social among the mothers, and they were not impressed with being interrupted or bossed about.

Everyone had taken their places—posted at gates leading to the pens for the nearest to motherhood and so forth while the remaining personnel mingled among the other mothers, trying to shuttle them to their destinations. Per Sam's standard instructions, "In" means this mother needs to go *into* the maternity pen, and "By" means the mother can wait and can go on by, down the alley to the awaiting pen.

Sam's expertise in identifying the physical readiness of the mothers made him the Grand Poobah "In" and "By" declarer, and the rest of the lot merely needed to do as instructed. They either opened the gate to the maternity pen or let her go on by. Personnel not posted at a gate were to assist in the "shooing" of the mother in the desired direction. Simple enough—cue the banjo and put it on fast forward.

The first five ladies to run the gauntlet were successfully "In'ed" and "By'ed" with additional credit to Brett for his efforts in talking the last two out of a hasty retreat toward the back of the corral where they could have ducked for cover and blended easily back in among the rest of the mothers. Kat and Axel were stationed at In and By gates respectively, leaving Brett and Kasi-Ann to direct the traffic.

The trouble was the traffic had no intention of cooperating. While the first five demonstrated the obstacle course, the remaining band had clearly taken the opportunity to devise a plan B and have themselves a right good giggle at the Pattersons' expense. Sam would send a cow toward the gate of choice, only to have her double back at the last second, causing Brett to jump to the nearest plank in the fence to keep from getting trampled. Next, they executed what looked like a cross between a box-and-chaser basketball defense and a glorified game of keep away. As Kasi-Ann would get one close to the gate, another would come along and make a run for the same gate, causing a break in the concentration just long enough that the first cow could then race back to the safety of the now-snickering mothers.

To add to the confusion, the chain closure on Kat's metal gate was banging out a mad bit of morse code from the constant thrusting open and jerking-shut reactions as the cattle darted toward her and then scattered. That round of Red Rover, Red Rover, sent Sam stomping on over.

Assuming this epic failure is because he is not in the primary position to move the mothers himself, he shoos Kasi-Ann out of the way and proceeds to deliver a litany of descriptive things that the gate help could do remedy the situation, including, but not limited to: Removal of certain body parts from other body parts regardless of whether or not this was actually physically possible, and "An anatomy lesson would *not* be required, *Kathryn;* thank you very much"—finishing breathlessly with the conveyance that all efforts produced on their part to present were a grievous and most untimely fiasco—And the thunder rolls.

Sam, whose shoulders were still heaving up and down from his impromptu State of the Union Address, turned back toward the cows. He was certain that this would bring everyone back to full attention as well as the task at hand. Somewhere amid the recommendations concerning body parts, Brett had joined Axel on the fence adjacent to his gate and began to take bets on exactly what shade of scarlet their mother's face could become before the smoke began to betray her eminent volcanic reply. She had visibly flinched at the emphasis put on the word *not* and her name during his speech but had yet, made no reply.

About the time they were collectively surmising that the entire episode was probably about as effective as bossing someone else's dog around, Kat soundlessly opened the gate and began to walk toward the house. Her once-laughing green eyes had turned a murderous shade of gray. The two boys drew their legs up further onto the fence as she walked past underneath them, muttering something about a high road, a test she hadn't studied for, and the prospect of someone going to heaven *today*. If needed, they could find her in the house stirring a crockpot that was somehow still in the pantry, but it was ill advised for at least another hour.

Sam was oblivious. Kasi-Ann had turned her attention to unraveling a length of discarded, rusty barbed wire she found coiled up next to the fence. The sleet that had been beating them in the face for the last hour had finally turned to snow in earnest, and the giant white flakes were beginning to stick.

Sam, now ready to have this rodeo at an end, had again begun pulling off specific mothers, sending them with their appropriate shouts of "In" and "By" over his shoulder while he faced the rest, holding them in position. He'd fix their little red wagons, by thunder.

After about ten or so mothers were sent without gates being operated, a fair queue had begun to form behind Sam. It wasn't until one of them ambled back up the alley toward him and stuck an inquisitive nose in his unsuspecting backside that Sam became aware of his suddenly reduced workforce. He shot an incredulous "what the dickens" glare at the boys who were still on the fence, now well into the second go in the best of three rounds of rock, paper, scissors to decide who was going to wade through disbanding mothers-to-be and tell their father that Mom had just submitted her two-week resignation, effective immediately.

All remaining sorting activities were thus adjourned until after lunch.

\*\*\*\*

Coming back to the present, Kat opened her eyes to find that she was, indeed, still in the corral and had not yet been delivered from evil. "I can do all things through Christ ..." she chanted soundlessly as the calves came boiling toward her gate. It was her last conscious thought as auto-pilot kicked in and she danced the back-and-forth dance with her clumsy gate for a partner. Kasi-Ann was dashing back and forth, half playing with the calves as she ushered them along, greeting each one with a "good morning" or salutation of some kind. Kat wasn't sure, but she thought she might have even heard her compliment one on the earrings they had chosen today, never mind that the red ear tags displaying each calf's number were all exactly the same. She cheerfully instructed them not to worry, that they would be back with their mommies soon. Kat couldn't help but smile at her daughter's easy kindness, and it reminded her of how much fun her family could have together.

Taking his cues from Kasi-Ann, Brett started playing the part of a personal escort for the mothers, adding "This way, madam, yes right in here... Yes, thank you for your patience. No ma'am, after you ..." Axel nearly succumbed to a fit of giggles as Brett practically hand-delivered them beyond his gate. Even the mothers, seemingly affected by the temporary spell, followed Brett, ceasing their distressed calls for their recently separated babes.

Brett could wear charm and charisma like a suit and tie, but Axel was usually responsible for miraculous favor with animals. He was the Critter Whisperer—didn't seem to matter how big, small, determined, or flighty the creature was. If Axel had time to be near and get quiet with them, they would be won over. It was a joy and a marvel to watch on most occasions. It was a downright frightening ordeal to witness when it involved snakes, skunks, porcupines, or otherwise unpopular creatures. However, this skill would not be required today as they made very short and light work of this round of sorting.

This was the usual Patterson way. They worked together; they played together.

CHAPTER 2

# The Branding

The entire two days prior had been spent on other branding preparations. Sam, Brett and Axel gathered horses and tack, branding irons, the stove to heat them, and other miscellaneous necessities. Kat and Kasi-Ann were on a mission to make enough food to feed a small army. In this country, friends and neighbors graciously helped one another out with no expectation of payment beyond a cool beverage, a hot meal and a warm handshake of thanks, knowing today they served the same neighbor who would come to serve them next week. The simple code was a commandment they found easy to live by.

The Pattersons would put forth a great spread, but nobody would think of arriving empty handed. The Five Loaves and Two Fish would multiply to astronomical proportions and *nobody* would be allowed to leave the ranch at the end of the day without taking leftovers home. Kat would go door to door of each vehicle, depositing zip lock bags and Tupperware if necessary, that would undoubtedly feed them well into the next week. The only other event that trumped the food production of a branding was a funeral, in which case the entire town suddenly became direct descendants of Betty Crocker.

Once again, as it often could, the branding this year fell on yet another Mother's Day. Kat had smirked as she stared at the spring flowers on the month of May page of their 2015 Stock Growers calendar, and written "Branding" on the Sunday Sam selected, thinking, *of course it is*.

Father's Day next month would find them fishing or taking in some other leisure activities, but Mother's Day somehow disappeared from the calendar under the weight of the letters "Branding" scrawled across it.

It was nothing short of a coming-on-the-clouds holy miracle that the sorting went as smoothly as could possibly be expected. The divorce lawyers on speed dial were laughingly let off retainer, and the morning sun was beginning to forecast a beautiful spring day.

Kat had just returned to the house as a loud, blaring horn announced the arrival of the first neighbors. Kat knew without looking it was Nancy Underwood, her fellow redhead and dear friend. She sounded a hearty good morning as the mudroom door opened. She was six feet tall, towering over Kat with her custom devil-may-care grin as she bent down to give her a hug.

"Happy Mother's Day, friend," she whispered. "Sam is fired again, I presume?" she asked stifling her Betty Rubble giggle as best she could without choking.

"Indeed," Kat qualified. "Or at least until he remembers to wish me Happy Mother's Day. My bet is noonish unless someone tips him off earlier," Kat remarked. As Kat was repaying the same well wishes of the day, Nancy's face became a mixture of inquisitive and mischievous.

"I'll see your noon, Kathryn Ann, and I'll raise you two hours," Nancy said with her little finger raised in front of Kat.

"The usual?" Kat inquired, raising hers. Nancy nodded in agreement.

"Done," Kat confirmed as she completed the traditional pinky promise/bet of $5, looking a bit impish herself.

After one last check on the multiple crockpots and roasters, Kat decided the army rations were well in hand, and they left the house to head back toward the corrals. Pickups and trailers were now filing in down the long driveway like a train, everyone hollering a greeting on their way by. Before long, a crew of thirty-five people and eight horses was assembled and ready for instructions. A pen of 250 calves, anxiously waiting for events of which they knew not, stared through the wooden slats at what was likely the largest assembly of humans they had ever seen. Across the corrals, in the back pasture, a congregation of concerned mothers, who knew full well the course of events that this day held, were pacing back and forth bellering.

The branding stove was lit while everyone finished their coffee and checked their gear. Kids were beginning to come out of the woodwork, climbing over fences and under gates, playing among the adults, begging for permission to go to the barn to see a new litter of kittens Kasi-Ann had told them about.

The younger ladies who were either inexperienced or not wishing to get dirty took their places perched on the fence to watch the others, a seemingly advantageous viewpoint. Folks with "years of experience" and the presence of mind to make better decisions about the extent of their physical participation were standing next to the branding stove with coffee cups in hand, ready to impart any wisdom they felt the younger generation might benefit from.

## The Branding

The first mishap occurred about fifty head in, which is miraculous really, when you consider the calf-to-horse-to-kid-to-vaccine needle-to-branding iron ratio, and the innumerable opportunities that presents for error on any of the aforementioned component's part. This one happened to be a loose horseshoe—child's play.

Axel was taking a turn roping, and his horse apparently felt inclined to jump at his shadow today—a curious improvement from this morning's earlier performance that included taking a complete leave of his senses after seeing his own reflection in a puddle.

The fright ended up requiring him to fully lay down to recover from the shock, however temporary it might have been. Axel had patiently held the lead rope with nothing more than a curiously inquisitive look in response.

Hazard was more than a fitting name for the tall, black-and-white paint horse. Sam would say he ought to skip the horse cake and give Hazard a little valium most of the time, shaking his head. He was shaking his head as Axel filled him in on the details of the shadow-boxing experience that resulted in the loose-fitting horseshoe that was now plaguing Hazard. Sam quickly took up the reins and headed Hazard for the barn where his shoeing tools were. The rest of the branding crew just filled in his spot, seamlessly charging forward.

A short time later, Kat and Nancy took the opportunity to go back to the house and check on the food and grab the coolers of beverages from the shop on their way back. They were just about to load the massive toolbox-sized coolers onto a red Honda 4-wheeler when they heard a rather loud expletive coming from the barn next door. As they entered the dusty building, they could hear Sam rifling in one of the stalls next to where his shoeing box and tools were located.

"Oh glory," Kat grumbled, knowing this was also the location of the vet box. Heaven only knew what manner of scrape, rip, tear, gouge, or partial severing Sam had encountered this time. What Kat did know, was that despite her nearly fifteen years in the medical field, she was the *last* person on the planet he would come to for first aid. He would consult his vet box to see what it had to offer presently, as the contents were generally subject to change without notice. Centuries-old cattle penicillin and a rusty old suture needle might be called upon to stitch up a limb if Kat were not around to speak sense and reason to him. That is, if he planned to do *anything* about the gaping wound that was currently drowning his boot with blood that was running down his elbow.

Sam had skillfully tapped in the first of three necessary horseshoe nails and was about to twist the pointed end off under the overturned hoof when Hazard realized he was not alone in the barn. A curious little black kitten with a splotch of white on her neck had arrived on the scene, and she was enthralled with his long swishing tail. Neither he nor Sam noticed her at first when she sat back on her back legs and tried swatting at the pendulous tail; however, she had Hazard's undivided attention when she caught it in mid-swing and decided to stay for the festivities. He jerked his hoof right through Sam's hand and up his arm trying to gain his feet and the nail scored a deep groove from the palm of his hand to his elbow. The subcutaneous fat layer beneath the skin was bulging out in the meaty portion of his hand, and by the time he reached the other end of the barn his forearm was covered in a warm, red river of blood.

## The Branding

"Great Gatsby, Samuel, what have you done!?" As a veteran nurse, she was not undone by the sight of blood or injury, but the extent of mishap that Sam could encounter never ceased to amaze her. She was about to engage in a single-sided argument—hers—regarding how he needed to observe proper care and cleaning methods, when he walked right past her and up to the house.

Incredulous, the girls followed him into the kitchen where he hung his arm over the sink and all but ordered Kat to rinse it. His eyes were beginning to glaze over a bit and cold sweat was dripping from his brow. Nancy quickly grabbed a dining room chair and set it down behind him. He already knew this one was out of his league, and they would be playing on her court today, however briefly, and he sat somewhat grudgingly onto the chair.

His manner told Kat he wasn't interested in hearing about the medical details, nor was she going to be given any great expanse of time to deal with it. While she irrigated the wound, she sent Nancy to fetch her medical bag from the bathroom cabinet. In twenty minutes time she had him cleaned, stitched from watch band to elbow crease, and dressed. The likelihood he would sit still for much longer was declining exponentially. It was no surprise to Kat when without a word, Sam marched back out to where Hazard was standing tethered in the barn and finished the job of securing the shoe, fully intending to proceed with the remainder of the day's work as well.

Hazard looked like he was mentally drafting a strongly worded letter to the ramrod of this outfit regarding the untimely and lengthy removal of himself from a branding that was just beginning to show some signs of excitement, but the kitten was still driving him to distraction, and he kept losing his train of thought.

As she watched him walking to the barn, Kat bit her lip resisting the urge to tell Sam to keep the bandage clean, and to take it easy so the stitches wouldn't split. She had made them small, using twice as many as she would on anyone else who would be even remotely compliant with post-suture instructions because it was a given that he would not. He really didn't mean to be obstinate where medical advice was concerned; he just had work to do, and failure was not an option.

As she stood mopping up the blood off the counter, Kat was still mildly in shock that he allowed her to tend the wound in the first place. She shook her head, making the transition from clinic back to ranch in her mind, remembering there was still a branding crew afoot. Nancy was already on it.

"Bless her heart," Kat murmured, a thankful smile gracing the corners of her mouth, as she watched her from the kitchen window.

She was already moving coolers from the shop to the corrals. By the time she arrived back on the scene, everyone had decided to take a few minute's break to refresh themselves and catch up on Sam's latest boo-boo. He was currently being elected President of the Bandage, Brace and Crutch Club from the sound of it, and she took the opportunity to steal a glance at the bandage while he was telling the castor of that electoral vote to take a long walk off a short bridge. It wasn't bleeding through—yet. *Thank the Lord,* she thought to herself. She had learned to take her victories as they were, no matter how small.

The branding was over half finished, and the crew was still in high gear, eager to complete the work. A short and thankfully uneventful time later found them sweaty, dirty, sporting the acquired fragrance strongly resembling singed hair, and *hungry*.

# The Branding

Tables and chairs had been set up in the shop for the branding meal. The long, narrow, wooden tool bench that took up over half of the back wall was covered with disposable tablecloths, ready to receive the buffet of goodies that was being marched in one by one. Crockpots and roasters, casserole dishes, and platters quickly took their places, filling the shop with a variety of mouth-watering aromas.

The children, who had been merrily running laps around the property for the last several hours, were now cropping up everywhere, professing their various states of starvation. Before too many hands had to be swatted away from the bounty, Sam and Kat asked for everyone's attention to give them their sincerest thanks for their treasured friendship and the help given today. With the blessing given, Axel had snatched a crusty roll in arguably the shortest response time from Amen to mouth on record.

Plates were filled and refilled as laughter echoed throughout the shop. Stories recounted the highlights of the day, catching Kat and Sam up on what they had missed.

It had turned into a glorious day. The warm, late afternoon rays of sun were streaming through the wide-open, large, double doors of the shop, accompanied by a refreshing light breeze. The birds were chirping in the nearby trees in agreement of "It Is Well."

An all-encompassing contentment settled on Kat as she looked around at her family and friends. These were without a doubt the greatest blessings in her life, upon which she could never hang a price tag.

Kat was pulled from her thoughts when Sam took her hand, leaned over, and kissed her gently on the cheek. He lingered there to whisper in her ear," Happy Mother's Day, love."

"Thank you, Sam," Kat said softly. She noted the time on her watch was 3 p.m. Then she hollered, "Nuts, Nancy, you win!" "Sam, do you have a $5?" she asked, laughing.

CHAPTER 3

# There's a Cow in My Room!

At 3:36 a.m., Kasi-Ann woke the entire household, wailing like a sinner. Kat had rounded the ornate wooden banister and scaled half of the staircase before the boys' doors just down the hall from Kasi-Ann's room had fully opened. Brett and Axel were both a mixture of concern and the bruised variety of dog tired from the branding. They offered no argument when Kat told them to return to bed.

Kat presumed this was yet another nocturnal adventure in Kasi-Ann's head where the events of the day came spilling back into the present regardless of how inconvenient the hour. She could be arguing with a cousin or one of her brothers—even a barn cat that she had found to be disagreeable earlier in the day. She found Kasi-Ann sideways in the middle of her bed tangled in the bed covers. She was still struggling when Kat gently shook her awake.

"Wake up, love, you're dreaming," Kat whispered softly. Kasi-Ann's eyes flew open at her mother's soothing voice. She immediately freed herself from the disheveled sheets and sat up, looking around.

"Where is it?!" she demanded.

"Where's what, dearest?" Kat asked, wondering to herself what the devil would have her so riled. She wasn't frightened; she was downright perturbed.

"The *cow!*" she shrieked in exasperation.

"Oh glory," Kat muttered under her breath, thinking of her clinic that would begin in a few short hours. *Would Kasi-Ann now be sorting in her sleep as well?*

"I promise you there are no cows here, honey, you can go back to sleep. It was nothing more than a dream," Kat added hoping she was awake enough to comprehend they were actually in conversation regarding whether or not there was a 1800-pound bovine kicking back in her 8 x12-foot room for the night.

"Well there had better *not* be," Kasi-Ann retorted very matter-of-factly. Resisting the urge to ask, "Or what, pray tell?" Kat eased her back onto the bed and began attempting a quick tuck in. She then decided on a diversion tactic.

"You were lots of help today, Kasi-Ann. Dad and I really appreciate everything you did. I'm sorry if it made you overtired and that you were working in your sleep," Kat said.

"It's not your fault, Mom," Kasi-Ann managed to say mid-yawn.

Kat gently kissed her forehead and said for the second time today her usual goodnight, "You are my greatest blessing, and I love you like the air I breathe." Exhausted, Kasi-Ann was asleep again in seconds, and Kat quietly left her room.

Sam was susceptible to the same episodes, complete with road rage when he had spent too many hours as a double agent in the cockpit of a semi on bovine relocation expeditions across the country. The fall run of cattle shipping was always the worst. His eyes would close, but the work continued on. He would thrash and talk in his sleep, and if you could make sense of what he was doing—driving in unrelenting traffic, loading or unloading the cattle, you could even manage to have a two-way conversation.

While Kat might have giggled a time or two at how the conversation turned out, ultimately, she always felt bad that he worked so hard all the time, only to be cheated out of well-deserved rest because his mind didn't get the memo to stop and rack out. Kasi-Ann worked and played just as hard with the same regrettable results.

As Kat descended back down the stairs, the recollection hit her like a ton of bricks. Kasi-Ann wasn't dreaming of the day's events—she was reliving the day Brett put a cow in her room!

Brett, maybe because he was older, always had more patience with Kasi-Ann, whether it was teaching or helping her to do something or just tolerating being in a hyperactive child's general presence. She had the unique ability to be so excitable she could hover a full foot off the ground for several hours at a time while simultaneously draining the energy and patience stores of anyone in a three-mile radius. Eventually even the dogs, loyal as the day is long, would slink off in search of a quiet spot to gather their wits and return their coats to the normal direction of growth.

One afternoon a few years back, Brett came rushing through the porch and mudroom doors into the kitchen, swiftly shutting and holding the door behind him. His expression resembled the picture of a man who was simultaneously being subjected to Chinese water torture and slowly being pecked to death by a chicken.

"She's driving me crazy, Mom!" Brett spewed, panting, half breathless from running the entire length of the driveway to ensure some distance between himself and his charge.

"She wants to argue with me about everything, and when she doesn't listen and just does things her own way, it ends up a disaster that I have to take time to fix!" he continued. "I've *had it*!" he added with a sigh and defeatedly slumped into a large log chair at the dining room table. By this time, Kasi-Ann had caught up and came bursting through the door. She wore the guilt of her foretold disagreeable behavior like a gunny sack.

"Brett's being rude, Mom!" she began in an attempt to plead her side of the case. Behind her, Kat practically heard Brett's eyes roll but declined turning around to witness whatever tacit reply he was exhibiting.

"Alright, enough—both of you," Kat said sternly. "Clearly this is just a case of Too Much Togetherness, and in my expert medical opinion, you should both go in exactly the opposite direction of one another until supper time. Now," she continued, "this sort of thing is highly contagious, and I don't want anyone else to be affected by it, so I will need you both to immediately go out of the house and take a walk. The breeze is perfect for blowing this kind of thing right off you. Brett, you go out to the stack yard, and on your way, make sure the ditch water level looks appropriate. Kasi-Ann, you go out to the mailbox and bring the post in please," Kat finished.

Kasi-Ann opened her mouth, likely to mention that she wasn't particularly in the mood to fetch the mail, when Brett cut her off, "Kasi-Ann, don't you dare backtalk Mom. I swear to heaven if you keep it up … I'm … I'm going to put a cow in your room!" he finally thundered, sounding a bit like it was the best he could come up with on short notice.

In truth, it really wasn't. In fact, it was the *best* threat he could have conjured up. Kasi-Ann was in the middle of scowling out an "Oh no, you won't" when Kat physically turned her around and escorted her out the door toward the mailbox. She stood and watched her kicking rocks down the driveway until she rounded the corner past the chicken coop and disappeared behind the trees of the apple orchard.

"Lord, this is a test I didn't study for ..." Kat murmured on her way back to the kitchen, wishing there was a manual given out on raising children, or even a Cliff's Notes version of some kind.

Brett hadn't been embellishing; she really was full-on today. But, as luck would have it, Kat had selected the best remedy for the ailment, and by the time everyone returned to the house, their attitudes were markedly improved.

Supper commenced without incident, and Kat had all but forgotten the events that had transpired earlier as her children were presently behaving dangerously close to humans. Kasi-Ann went off to take a shower, and the rest of the family settled in the living room. The stairway to the upstairs bedrooms where the children slept happened to be adjacent to the living room and right over top of the downstairs bathroom. As soon as Brett heard the water of Kasi-Ann's shower turn on, he flew into action. He opened and slammed the back-porch door and began stomping up the stairs, beating on the walls, and making enough racket to raise the dead. "Here, get along there!" he hollered.

"Get on up there!" "Sssssssss!" He thundered and carried on like he was herding cattle up the stairs—and that was when Kat remembered Brett's vehement promise.

Having a front row seat to Brett's exhibition, Sam looked questioningly at Kat for an explanation to their eldest son's sudden onset of apparent witlessness. Kat just shook her head at him, wordlessly telling him not to ask.

It was common knowledge within the family that Kasi-Ann was still more than a little bit intimidated by the stock, and the thought of having a cow in her room had to be a living nightmare. Brett, undoubtedly, was banking on it. He'd even gone as far as to go online and download an angry-sounding cow mooing loudly for additional effect.

The computer room where they did their homework was at the top of the landing and right across the hall from Kasi-Ann's room. He'd have the perfect vantage point to view the whole thing.

Brett was sitting sideways in the oversized leather recliner, his leg lazily bobbing up and down when Kasi-Ann came through the living room in her fluffy pink camo robe headed for her room.

"I put number 57 in your room by the way," he mentioned casually as she passed, as normally as you might say *goodnight* or *see ya later.*

Number 57 happened to be known for being a particularly ill-tempered cow that would charge you as soon as look at you. Sam favored the word *trashy* as her general description, and that was being generous. Her red ear tag bearing the number 57 was more like a criminal number seen on a mug shot.

That struck a chord. Kasi-Ann immediately stopped and stiffened, then whirled around, reverting to defiant mode in the space of a nanosecond.

"No, you didn't!" she fired back, riveted to her spot.

"I did," Brett began tauntingly, "I said I would, and I did. Didn't you hear me shoving her up the stairs?"

"That was just you making a noise," Kasi-Ann retorted, but Brett hadn't failed to miss that she still was yet to budge an inch toward going upstairs.

"C'mon, Axel, let's go see how many of her papers she's chewed up," Brett teased, finishing with a comment regarding whether this particularly unruly cow might want to sleep in Kasi-Ann's bed.

Well, that did it. She was right behind them scurrying up the stairs until all three of them were standing outside her closed bedroom door. Kat, fearful that a referee might be required, was nearing the top of the stairs as well just as the formidable shouting match ensued. Amid the "no, you didn'ts" and "yes, I dids," Sam was shocked to hear Kat's usually soft voice shouting over the top.

"Judas Priest, enough, all of you!" Kat bellowed. "Kasi-Ann, I'll open the door myself ..." She said, trailing off.

Just then something mischievous overthrew Kat's better judgment, and she decided to play along. Meanwhile, Brett had already backed up, taking position in the computer room, and cranked up the speakers. Kat gingerly cracked the door open and began to peer inside.

"Sweet merciful heaven, there *is* a cow in there!" she squealed as she abruptly pulled the door shut again.

Kasi-Ann couldn't believe her ears. Moreover, she couldn't believe she was about to open the door and look for herself, but she felt her hand on the knob, and it was turning—with a small click the door opened and she stuck one wide eyeball up to the space between the door jamb and the door.

About that time Brett hit play on the recording and the would-be Number 57 let out a roar that would have curled Sam's hair. Kasi-Ann quit the landing and was off like a shot. If her feet had touched a single stair, she would have suffered a tuck and tumble with no recovery, but there was nothing but air under her until she was at the bottom of the staircase going through the back porch door, across the backyard, and clean out into the hay field.

Brett was on his knees in a fit of hypoxic hysteria, deprived of both words and proper oxygen for a full five minutes before he could gather himself enough to go and find her. He knew he owed her some sort of an apology, but it would simply have to wait for ensuing hiccups to subside. Kat had to sit down on the stairs to keep from careening down them as her own laughter filled the hallway. Downstairs, Sam sat in his chair staring up at them, somewhat blinking in disbelief, as though they had all decided to dye their hair blue.

Eventually Brett went to find Kasi-Ann, and they had a long talk about how he was responsible for her when Mom and Dad were not around and that she needed to listen to him just like she listens to them when they are in charge. They settled their differences, and then Brett let her in on an important secret—about how most of the time, the cows are more scared of her than she is of them. This theory, however, was absolutely *not* to be tested on No. 57.

Honor thy father and mother—and sometimes your brother.

## CHAPTER 4

# Everyone Has a Goliath

The following day was Monday. It was Kasi-Ann's least favorite day of the whole week. It was not because there wasn't any school on the weekends or that Mondays marked the beginning of another work week. It was because every Monday she had to face Crankenstein.

Curtis James Bevolden, the Patterson's elder neighbor of decades, was her own personal giant, standing between her and the Promised Land, and she had brought a rock to a swordfight.

Sometime ago he had agreed to an arrangement of looking after Kasi-Ann on Monday afternoons from the time she got off the school bus to when either of her parents got home. Kat had a late clinic in town on Monday evenings, and Sam could be anywhere trucking cattle or engaged in other ranch business. Her older brothers were more than capable of looking after their younger sister, however Kat felt this was a more suitable arrangement that allowed them time to do their homework and chores without the additional burden of babysitting.

Kasi-Ann would have visibly flinched at that particular choice of vocabulary because babysitting implied she was a baby, and she could satisfactorily mind herself at the ripe old age of seven, thank you very much. Just ask her, and she would tell you. It was one of the many areas in which she could be rather opinionated for one so small. This, however, was still an improvement over daycare, which Kasi-Ann had decided was simply a jail with finger painting. Kindergarten had scarcely been a rung above daycare, however additional credit had been awarded for the lack of forced naps.

The reddish highlights that would betray her blondish-brown hair in the summer sun came straight from her mother, cleverly attached to the "feisty" gene, Sam would say as long as Kat was out of earshot. It was something you didn't see outright, but in time, it would eventually be unearthed, and likely by that time, it was too late.

From the time she learned to walk, she was determined to be first, even if it meant knocking Kat or anyone else who stood in the way down the remaining stairs to arrive at the bottom before them. Kat chose to see this as drive instead of an episode of impoliteness, and believed fervently that it would take her daughter every step of where she wanted to go in life, even if it kept her mother on her knees for most of it.

Crankenstein actually got a kick out of Kasi-Ann. She was fearless. Where other small children would cower at his deep voice, she would bow her neck and fire back. He rather appreciated her determined attitude and quick wit, but he especially enjoyed that he could sufficiently ruffle her feathers inside a few minutes. It was a game they would play, whether she knew she was playing or not, and she was always quick to participate. With a simple comment on the day's weather, he could engage her, and the battle of wits was on.

As Mr. Bevolden sat on the porch swing of the towering, white ranch house waiting for the school bus coming down the long winding driveway, he studied the blossoming trees of the apple orchard. Today the air was fragrant with memories. He had watched Sam playing in this same orchard as a child whenever he had come to lend his father a hand.

Kasi-Ann was much like Sam in her love of being outside. Inclement weather simply meant a change in whatever you were wearing outside because staying inside was simply unthinkable. To clarify, this refers to being inside the house, as being inside one of the barns is clearly a different matter entirely. Either way, Kasi-Ann seemed to be oblivious to the cold and seldom had on appropriate clothing for the given weather.

He chuckled to himself as he looked across the driveway, towards the barn, at a couple of the large mud puddles that had formed in the low spots. Several years ago, on one of the first occasions he'd had to look after Kasi-Ann, the spring rains had left behind some similarly scattered bodies of water. She had emerged from the house wearing shorts with a pair of rubber chore boots and holding an umbrella, though it had not been raining at the time. Mr. Bevolden was an active man, always preferring to be doing something useful, so they were outside in the yard where he would be trimming the yard hedge as they passed the time.

She had certainly inherited her father's "Water Baby" gene, Kat would say, as long as Sam was out of earshot—and she had spotted the large puddles the moment they arrived outside. She would have had anyone believe that they actually called to her, extending an invitation she simply couldn't resist, much as the sea beckons the return of the mermaid.

She was on her way down the driveway when Mr. Bevolden called out to her to stay where he could see her and to keep out of mischief. The only effect declaring his true meaning (keep yourself clean and dry) would have had, would be to decrease the number of circles around the puddles she walked before splashing straight in, but he was truly ill prepared for the response his repeated requests would illicit. Despite his most recent stern command for her to get away from the puddles, she hedged closer and closer, dipping a now fully defiant toe into the murky brown water, as she stared at him across the yard.

Their eyes met. The theme song from *The Good, the Bad and the Ugly* all but whistled through the cottonwood trees. They squinted at one another. He set the clippers down on top of the hedge and put his hands on his hips, fiercely staring back at her. She swirled her toe around in the puddle.

Seeing this had not produced the desired effect, he began to make his way to where she stood at the puddle's edge. Feeling sure this gesture would invoke enough fear for her to quit her puddle hopping and come back to the yard, he continued toward her with renewed enthusiasm. Her response floored him. Her hands flew to her little hips, and she began to match his determined stare like a showdown at the OK Corral. She didn't budge. A lone tumbleweed tiptoed across the expanse of dirt driveway remaining between them. Still he marched—still she glared.

"I *told* you to stay out of that water, Kasi-Ann," he barked, swallowing up the distance between them with every long stride.

Still she held her ground. Her face was scowling now, her little eyebrows knitted together. He was now just a foot away from her, and beyond proper cross. He opened his mouth to deliver her a last chance to comply, when she threw her arms in the air and flung herself backwards in reckless abandon, landing straight in the middle of the deep puddle. She was completely immersed for a second, and then came back to the top, floating and smugly performing snow angels as he gasped in disbelief. That lasted only a moment.

Suddenly, he was furious—so much so that he could only sputter, as any real words evaded him. About the time she rolled over onto her tummy and began attempting a breaststroke, he swooped down and plucked her out of the puddle by the seat of her shorts. Making no genuine effort to fight, she went limp as he hauled her under one arm, dripping and muddy, all the way to the porch.

It was not the warmest spring day, but he made her stand there in the grass while he readied the garden hose on the side of the house. He turned the water on her, expecting her to squeal from the cold, but instead, she danced around, singing as the muck was rinsed off.

Technically, she had won, as wet was all she wanted to be in the first place—muddy had just been a bonus. The sparkle had found its way back to her eyes as he finished, and he couldn't help but laugh at how she delighted in being a drowned rat. He even let her stand under the shower of the hose with her umbrella for a few minutes as a peace offering. He then sent her to the house for some dry clothes, and he stared after her almost disappointedly when she gave no argument. He returned somewhat bewildered to his hedge trimming. This little opinionated bit of goods was certainly more than he'd bargained for.

The cheerful beep-beep of the bright yellow school bus pulling up brought him from his daydream as the prisoner filed off and stood to face her warden.

"Crank-," she began and abruptly changed, "er ... Mr. Bevolden," Kasi-Ann corrected, observing her parents' uncontested rules of respect, her face battle ready.

"Kasi-Ann," he returned, with matched intensity. "Looks like a good day for a dip ... what do you think?" he asked in a voice that was dripping with "I-double-dog-dare-you." She took the bait hook, line, and sinker, just as he knew she would.

Camo Girl

CHAPTER 5

# Camo Girl

Kat arrived home from her evening clinic a bit earlier than usual. As she expected, Kasi-Ann and Mr. Bevolden were engaged in a mini-debate over something upon her arrival. Kasi-Ann was so busy pleading her case to Mr. Bevolden that she hadn't even noticed her mother's car in the driveway.

Kat had stopped to water the flower beds in the backyard and could hear their discussion. Kasi-Ann was helping with supper preparations as she often did and was doing her best to convince Mr. Bevolden that she could lift the large roaster pan out of the oven herself. After all, she was going to be a chef someday, she had reasoned, as though this was qualification enough to safely hoist the enormous Dutch oven from the inferno.

When she was finally convinced she was getting nowhere with her arguments, she resigned herself to setting the table. She was carefully setting the flatware when her mother emerged through the back-porch door.

"It smells divine, Mr. Bevolden. What culinary miracle have you planned for us this evening?" Kat asked.

"Sunday pot roast, mashed potatoes and gravy and tender baby carrots, my lady," he answered, all but beaming with pride.

"Sunday pot roast on a Monday? Indeed, Mr. Bevolden, you are quite the rebel. What will the neighbors say?" Kat teased.

"Let them rattle," he replied, a sly smile tugging at the corner of his mouth.

Admitting to himself that down deep, although he rather did enjoy the notion of stirring the local busybodies, he decided it would likely require a greater effort than the pot roast offense in question. On second thought, that might not be entirely true either.

He put that thought aside to tend his gravy properly as Kat sent Kasi-Ann to the barns in search of her brothers. Axel met her halfway up the drive, declaring that his nose was reporting mashed potatoes to his stomach and his stomach was asking why they hadn't been reported to his mouth yet.

Given the opportunity, Axel could probably eat his own weight at a single setting, no doubt storing it in his long lanky limbs. Kat often inquired where he put it all. He would easily be as tall as Sam, maybe even taller.

Mr. Bevolden stayed to dine with the family and clean up while Kat ushered Kasi-Ann through washing up and getting ready for bed. Since his wife's passing, he had seldom felt useful. When Kat first suggested the Monday afternoon arrangement, it was simply something to do with his time. Since then, it had blossomed into the one day of the week he looked forward to the most. Squaring off with Kasi-Ann kept his mind sharp. The meal he prepared and shared with them was the best and often the only company he kept all week outside of Sunday services.

The fact that he needed the Pattersons as much as they needed him escaped none of them, but it was a conversation that did not require words to explain itself. Loss and grief had undoubtedly brought them closer together than neighboring property.

Upstairs Kat was listening to Kasi-Ann's 100 mph recounting of her day while she held up clothing selections for tomorrow's prospective school attire. Kasi-Ann had wrinkled her nose and shook her head for a third time now at the choices for pants, so Kat gestured for her to come pick something herself. When she was of a mind to be difficult she was 100 percent committed, and Kat had learned to recognize when to quickly choose her battles. Clean and dry would outrank matching and sometimes even properly fitting when it came right down to the nitty gritty of it.

As Kasi-Ann came to the dinner preparation portion of her day, she filled her mother in on how she was not allowed to remove the big pan from the oven.

"I know he didn't want me to get burned, Mom, but I'm not a baby," she said a bit more poutily than her recent exclamation could justify.

Looking forward to her nightly story, she looked up suddenly exclaiming, "Camo Girl could have done it! She probably would have roped it and dragged it out and never spilled a thing!"

From the time Kasi-Ann was quite little, Kat had made a nightly tradition of telling her stories in which she was the hero. Being raised with two rough and rowdy older brothers, she was forever wanting to be just like them, doing what they were doing, going where they were going. By the age of four being called a "Girl" was about the foulest name you could have used and considered "fightin' words." Kat did her best to keep a little "pink" in her world despite all the tomboy tendencies. Because the boys wore camo shirts, so did she—but Kat would make sure hers was pink. And Camo Girl was born. She had pink camo pajamas, bedding, t-shirts, ball caps, even a set of pink camo saddle bags with her brand stitched on them.

She told Kasi-Ann stories about how Camo Girl was the fastest riding, straightest shooting and toughest girl in all of Montana—and she was *not* afraid to wear pink! In fact, she wasn't afraid of anything—and it had served her well in the face of everything from broccoli to the first day of school.

It was Kat's intention to draw every parallel between Camo Girl and Kasi-Ann that she could until, like Peter Pan's shadow, she stitched her into the very fiber of the little girl's being, with no discernible indication where one stopped and the other began. Kat's greatest hope was that one day Kasi-Ann would understand that the superhero qualities and can-do power mentality were always on the inside of her, and there wouldn't be anything she couldn't accomplish if she set her mind to it.

Kat brightened, agreeing with Kasi-Ann, and produced a story of how Camo Girl had yet again done such amazing things, saving the day, all the while Kasi-Ann was hanging on Kat's every word. There were moments where she looked up thoughtfully, no doubt picturing herself performing the heroic feats. They finished the story time with prayers, and then Kat hugged Kasi-Ann and bid her good night.

CHAPTER 6

# The Upside-Down Trail

One evening after supper, Sam sat at the sprawling log dining room table, plotting. The spring had tumbled head long into summer. Somewhere between the end of school and the beginning of the warm weather sport, the Patterson family affectionately called haying, a month had evaporated into thin air.

The first cutting of hay usually began around the Fourth of July, effectively making travel for the holiday impossible. By the time the entire acreage was all swathed and laying on the ground drying, that which was cut first was nearly ready for baling. If the weather was cooperative, it was paramount to proceed with the process to ensure the best bales—hence the phrase "make hay while the sun shines."

Sam did his best to scratch out an afternoon of leisure here and there, usually a float down the Yellowstone River to appease his inner water baby. It was a refreshing activity the entire family could partake in to beat the often relentless Montana summer heat. The elevation seemed to allow the sun to sit right on top of one's shoulders, and a few hours of relaxation on the cool water was a welcome respite. It was times like this that Kat desperately prayed for rain. It was the only way to make Sam come to a complete stop for more than five hours at a time.

After the first cutting of hay was baled and the bales were all moved and stacked in the stack yard, it would simply begin all over again. Moving irrigation water would again become the morning and evening chore that tugged at their sleeves like an antsy toddler needing to find a restroom. They would go through cans of Deep Woods Off like an '80s beauty salon used hairspray, fighting off some of the larger crop with shovels when necessary. The mosquitoes that lived along the ditch were almost big enough to stand flat-footed and see eyeball to eyeball with a turkey.

Kasi-Ann's usual lack of appropriate clothing would earn her enough bites in a single outing to pass for measles, until Kat could bathe her in oatmeal and Bactine.

Each of them stood on the promise that as soon as the haying was completed, they might get to go camping—and not just the version that amounted to the overnight tossing up of a nylon tent in the backyard, though Kasi-Ann would argue that this was still quite agreeable under most circumstances. Camping to this family of five was a major event. Never mind that it was the only kind of vacation they had ever been on—but it would take days of careful planning and amassing of necessary items, as well as the readying of multiple animals. The Pattersons would be packing into the mountains on horseback, with a pack string of giant draft-crossed mules. Everything would need to be carefully weighed and loaded evenly over the pack animals, and only the bare essentials above food and lodging would be brought along. Sam could get highly creative with his packing skills, filling out loads with things like canned goods or flashlights to make sure everything was accounted for and perfectly balanced. A large, mostly white, canvas wall tent would serve as the portable Patterson Hilton, requiring long poles to be cut from downed timber upon arrival and erected as an A frame to support the structure.

A Patterson family vacation might be comparable by most other people's standards to a week-long visitation to Alcatraz, complete with experiences that even a life sentence of therapy could not undo. But there was something magical and almost surreal that happened when Sam stepped off the grid, and the veil of trees filled in behind him. It sealed an unseen door from the everyday world and the one Kat witnessed each time they were afforded the luxury of time enough to go.

It was as though time halted and then ran backwards, erasing years, even decades. Sam was an old soul, seemingly born a century too late. In the middle of the wilderness, he was in his natural element, and never closer to God than any other place on earth. His body would visibly relax, every cellular component of his person sighing contentedly and gratefully, like someone returning home from a long and wearisome journey. He was always acutely aware of everything in their surroundings, knowing it all by smell, sound, or sight. He knew it like he knew the marks of his own hand because it too was a part of him—part of the breath in his lungs and the very beating of his heart. There was a part of him that only lived there, ever waiting patiently for his return, when for a short time, he could be completely whole. It was where he knew his greatest happiness. No phones, no work schedules, no worldly cares—only earth and sky that man had not yet contaminated.

From the moment that Sam committed to "going on vacation," the work began. Each horse and mule had to have their hooves trimmed and/or be shod. A couple of the daily drivers would either need new shoes or at the very least an inspection for general hoof and overall health. Sam was not about to take any chances with the lives or limbs of his family or his stock. He treated every animal with genuine respect and care. His father had drilled it into him that being a good steward of all that he was entrusted with was as necessary as breathing and should, thus, be just as involuntary—something you never had to be reminded to do. It was something he passed on to his children with the same passion, and they each had their own fondness for the animals they cared for.

With horse cake in their hands and back pockets, Sam and the boys gathered all the horses and mules, tethering them to the long wooden hitching rail in front of the large central barn. The mules stamped and pawed at the gravel impatiently, apparently wanting more cake. They would follow you for miles chasing the delicious scent of this favorite treat, and there was no better assurance of being able to catch any of them in the mountains at a moment's notice if need be.

Sam thought better of inspecting the horses first and decided if he wanted to avoid any additional potholes out front he'd best tend to the giants first. They were all mostly well-mannered aside from a little impatience and trench-digging tendencies, so Sam had them tidied up in relatively short order. Abigail, or Abby, stood the tallest, and her jet black, younger, twin siblings Cross and Calvary were only a slight inch or two shorter for the time being. Even Sam who was well over six and a half feet tall seemed dwarfed, standing among these massive mules. He mused that he could probably sling a Volkswagen on either side of them if he could manage to get it hoisted that high.

The last was a mini mule. Sabbath was actually just of normal size, but next to the rest she looked like a sorrel, teacup-sized, toy replica. On the inside, she acted like she was just as big as the rest, and in her heart she was. Kat could appreciate that from one fiery, short-statured, red-haired girl to another.

Hitler Cat, the barn's confirmed bachelor, was sizing them all up with a look of disdain from the ajar hayloft door directly above. His manner was a mix of smug and disgusted. He was black with white on his chest and face, and an odd bit of black above his mouth that looked distinctly like a small mustache. This coupled with his lofty opinion of himself and general lack of opinion for everyone else had earned him his name. He kept to himself mostly, simply a spectator of the goings on, except for the rare occasions when Axel's spell drew him in, even if only for a moment.

He was currently studying Sam scratching Calvary's ears with more curiosity than he'd care to admit to. Before the notion to wonder what that might feel like got the better of him, he settled himself onto a beam for a nap, forgetting all of them with a simple swish of his sleek black tail.

Munching their sweet reward, the towering trio was ushered into their spacious individual stalls to wait for the remainder of the herd.

Next came Delilah, Kat's strawberry roan, and Sam's chestnut thoroughbred Damascus. As lord and lady of the daily driver team, they were up-to-date in all manner of upkeep and received only a visual once over and complementary brush down for their trouble. Had anything further been necessary for Damascus, a pre-game warm-up would have been required.

Damascus was as hard-headed as Sam, perhaps slightly more so if that were genuinely possible. He and Sam had established quite some time ago that if Damascus wanted to buck Sam off, he could, and there would be little to be done about it, regardless of Sam's extensive horse experience and riding ability. It was this experience that led Sam to believe they were much the same—each willing the other to see it their way, and on the occasional day when Damascus flat refused to yield, Sam would have to take his turn, generally in the willows—or whatever terrain presented itself at the time of the overthrow. And then for a time, there would be peace in the valley yet again.

The final lineup contained Kasi-Ann's faithful mount Pentecost, who was usually just called Penny. She had practically helped raise Brett and Axel, and now was Kasi-Ann's four-legged nursemaid. She had been bomb proof from the day she was born and was immediately crowned "the kid horse." Sam trimmed her feet and expertly fitted her with four new size 00 shoes, tidied her mane for the bridle, and treated her to a brushing for her usual good behavior.

Brett and Axel, already possessing a lifetime membership at the Patterson Livery, were seeing to their own horses and gear. Brett's dapple gray horse Caesar stood almost ceremoniously tall and still for the duration that he was worked over, while Hazard, Axel's ADD problem child danced and ducked at every small movement in his general vicinity. He suspiciously followed a passing butterfly with half crossing eyes until his nose bumped into Caesar. He simply viewed the interruption with an annoyed snort, then with a royal dismissal of the "peasant agitation," resumed his tall, aloof, rather quite-better-than-you, posture. In truth, Caesar really was somewhat of a snob, but as luck would have it, Hazard, who was somehow predestined to be the court jester, was too much of an idiot to notice.

The boys, finished with their preparations, put the horses in their respective stalls and headed for the shop to begin the next chore on the to-do list. This meant finding Sam and asking what they should do next. Kat could have lists of lists posted on the refrigerator at any given time, but Sam only ever kept a mental inventory.

Sam was just bringing Solomon round to the barn where the rest were enjoying their cake and grain. Solomon had been his father's horse. He was too old now for a trip to the mountains, too old for much of anything really, but Sam didn't have the heart to let him go just yet. He lived out a life of ease, pasturing close to the ranch where he was looked after. Sam escorted the patriarch to his usual stall and served up his favorites. He would be glad of the afternoon company even if he would not get to go along. Both boys greeted him and scratched his ears and neck while he ate, until Sam reminded them they needed to keep moving.

At the right of the entrance of the large red barn was a separate room where all the saddles and tack were kept. Sam opened the wooden door and headed for the back wall of shelves. He pulled down two bright orange panniers, handing them off to the boys behind him. He repeated the exercise with a matching brown set. These hard plastic boxes would be loaded with all of their supplies along with some soft-sided versions that Sam was currently searching for. The orange set had legs that screwed into the bottom so that they could be elevated from the ground, hooking together by the lids to create an upright table or work surface. Almost everything that went to the mountains was dual purpose.

Most of everything they needed was already stored in the panniers to make for quick packing, but Sam always went through them carefully, checking off his mental list to be sure they had everything. The mountains were not a place to find you left something important at home, and by the time they left, they were usually successfully overpacked to the point that Sam would say, "*If we don't have it, we don't need it.*"

In the house, Kat and Kasi-Ann were busy with food preparations for their trip. Years of practice had taught them many lessons about what was easy to pack and keep cold, fresh, or intact enough to survive the journey. Whenever any questions arose, Sam was the resident expert and usually the final decision on the matter, as he was the one who ultimately had to figure out how and where to pack it.

The dining room table was covered in pantry items to be loaded this evening and the cold items would be packed with blocks of ice in the morning, last thing before they left. Sam and the boys had just arrived with the packs for the food as Kat crossed the last item off her last list.

Sam looked at the amount of food on the table and looked back at Kat, exasperated at her built-in ability to overpack for one so small.

"Dearest, we are going for less than a week, not a month," he said, with extra emphasis on the word *dearest*, and then trailed off, knowing better than to begin a quarrel at this particular juncture in their packing endeavors.

"I'll do my best to get everything I can in there," he quickly filled her silent response with.

Kat giggled at his obvious discomfort and hollered back over her shoulder to select whatever he wanted and felt was best as she headed out the back-porch door toward the BBQ grill in preparation of grilling steaks. If there had been anything truly particular that she desired to have, she needed only to let him know, and he'd have moved heaven and earth to do it for her, and she knew it. Right now, she wanted nothing more than to have everything packed and loaded in the horse trailer so they could sit down and enjoy a nice dinner together after the long day of preparations.

She knew Sam didn't like to reheat a steak, so he would be prompt for dinner, but he would not come in until the work was done either because once he ate, his gumption got overruled by digestion. She turned the flame down low to let the grill heat slowly and challenged them to an impromptu race.

"Last one to the barn is a rotten egg!" she shouted as she dashed through the kitchen and out the mud room door.

Axel reacted immediately, stepping on Sam's foot under the table in the process of making his way toward the door. Brett caught him around the waist in an attempt to pull him back, and they tumbled to the kitchen floor in a ball as Kasi-Ann pulled out some football moves, skirting around and swatting away an outstretched hand meant to pull her into their rolling wreck. They each tried to wrestle free of each other, then finally scrambled to their feet and were in hot pursuit of her a few moments later. Sam was already out the back-porch door, heading around for the side door located at the back of the barn. Kasi-Ann flew across the driveway as fast as her little legs would carry her, executing a Dukes of Hazard General Lee launch, complete with slow motion hang time, landing in Kat's arms at the wide-open barn door. The boys came thundering in on her heels, Axel barely a breath ahead of Brett. They looked up expecting Sam to be right behind them, but he wasn't.

Mildly disappointed, Kat figured he was too tired by this time of day for her little game and that he'd be along directly, so she started toward the back of the barn to open the other doors and allow a little more air flow.

Just then, Sam emerged from the last stall and shouted "Gotcha!" and grabbed Kat around the waist, twirling her around.

She screamed like the devil himself had her by the hair until she gathered her wits enough to realize it was Sam. The squealing turned into laughter as he continued spinning her around in a circle. The death grip she had on his head eased, and her arms were around his neck now, her face flushing from both the fright and laughter.

They were both dizzy when he set her back on her feet, the creaking of the barn wood floor his only real assurance she was safely on the ground. Holding onto her shoulders, he had looked at her a long moment before his ocean blue eyes finally focused and fixed on hers. He gave her a little squeeze, and then he cocked his head thoughtfully.

"You're mighty pretty when you're scared, ma'am," he whispered, gently letting go of her and making his way to the front doors.

Her cheeks bore a true blush now. All she could do was stare after him, dazed and trying to maintain her own footing. Heaven bless it, that man could undo her with a simple smile, and the criminal knew it.

"Alright enough foolin' about, you lazy saddlebums; let's get this gear loaded," Sam said playfully, as he headed to pull the horse trailer up in front of the barn.

He paused a moment to add, "And you, sir, are a rotten egg," he said grinning at Brett and stepped out the barn door.

A shiny, gun-metal gray, flatbed Ford F350 was hitched to the long gooseneck Donahue trailer, waiting about fifty yards down the driveway. Sam whistled cheerfully as he walked, reflecting on the day, and his excitement for the upcoming trip.

They had everything loaded and packed just about the time the boys' stomachs began betraying them. Sam was walking in between them down the dusty driveway on their way back to the house and was beginning to wonder if they weren't having a conversation back and forth. Kat was throwing giant T-bone steaks on the grill a scant five minutes later, and the aroma was enough to overthrow a devout Catholic the first Friday of Lent.

"I bet those are gonna be good enough to make you take back stuff ya never did steal!" Sam remarked, peering over Kat's shoulder. "If you boys will go and bring that patio table up here where there's more shade, we'll eat out here tonight," Sam said.

They brought the glass-top table from the center of the backyard closer to the back porch and Kasi-Ann began bringing the chairs. Kat brought out the plates and silverware and went back in after the rest of the food. Kasi-Ann was just setting the last place as the salad and fruit made their way out to the table, and Sam was assembling steaks on a large, oval, glass platter.

He had just set them down as everyone else began to be seated, but he had one last requirement. He dashed over to the far corner of the yard where a few remaining rogue dandelions had survived the last Roundup raid, and reaching under the bottom string of the barbed wire fence, plucked a couple of the fat, yellow flowers.

Returning to the table, he held them out, smiling at Kat. "For the lady of the house," he said with a small bow, and her blush was back right on cue. It occurred to him that he was the only one still standing, and he did something then that he had never done.

It was his father that said the blessing before a meal as Sam was growing up, and he customarily would stand with his hand on his mother's shoulder as he spoke. Only after this was done would he take his seat and everyone would eat.

He could not give an explanation as to why, but he felt so strongly compelled to do it that before he knew what he was about, his eyes were closed, and he began giving thanks. He felt Kat's hand come to rest on his that was lightly sitting atop her shoulder, and he knew without words that she understood the significance. Heaven knows she had been a guest at his family's table most of her life.

The children, being accustomed to the fact that their parents were prone to random fits of prayer, transitioned easily to a bowed head and folded hands regardless of the circumstances. If it was a lengthy prayer, Axel transitioned quickly from bowed head and folded hands to snoring and drooling.

Finishing, Sam took his seat and silently looked around the table at his family as they passed the food laughing and talking. He was suddenly aware that he was starving, and so very blessed.

Kasi-Ann was so stoked to finally be going camping, she was the first one up and was excited to show everyone that she had made the coffee. Kat had heard the ruckus in the kitchen and had come to her aid before she toppled off the heavy log chair she had scooted the entire length of the kitchen to stand in front of the coffee pot.

Juggling the full carafe of water to be poured into the Bunn coffee maker, she was attempting to crawl up onto the chair just as Kat emerged on the scene. Knowing how much she really wanted to help, and to do it herself naturally, Kat merely suggested that she set the pot on the countertop first, and then climb up. Seconds later, hot see-through coffee was filling the pot. Thankful for the swiftness of this particular coffee pot, Kat sent Kasi-Ann to wake her brothers and scrambled to make another pot before Sam had to apologize for any kind of unsolicited coffee critiques.

Breakfast-to-go came in the form of breakfast burritos that Kat had made the day before, and it was being escorted to the pickup less than twenty minutes later. The boys had all but raced down the stairs and straight to the barn to begin saddling up horses. The dust of "vacation has begun," started to fly out behind them inside another forty-five minutes. It was now 5:02 a.m.

It was approximately fifty-five miles to the trailhead by way of interstate, then county road, and eventually an hour and a half of the finest washboard infested, winding, forest-service dirt tax dollars could buy. It had potholes large enough to lose a Jeep Wrangler in. That was, if you didn't bounce off the road completely and end up parked in the rhubarb. In the end, you would eventually find yourself parked in the rhubarb as there was no real designated parking area by the trailhead.

Brett and Axel had all but inhaled their burritos and then proceeded to sleep for the remainder of the ride. Kasi-Ann giggled as they jostled around in the backseat, occasionally banging their heads together, but it did not elicit a coherent response from either of the slumbering youths.

By Kat's watch, it was exactly a quarter of an hour past a second lapsing of bumpy eternity when Sam finally pulled off the dilapidated excuse of a road and parked the trailer. The brilliant, orange, sunrise set across the backdrop of mountains had been breathtaking, but Kat was sure she was the only one who had truly appreciated it.

The boys were awake immediately, stirred by the sudden stillness. There was a short flurry of hat grabbing and jockeying for position that quickly tumbled out the back doors, somehow managing to land on their feet.

Sam opened the backdoor of the trailer and began leading horses out. The mules were in the front of the trailer, staring out eye level from the opening at the upper portion of the sides, giving them the appearance that they were wearing the trailer as some sort of costume. They were keenly surveying the new scenery but appeared content to wait their turn to be liberated.

The three dogs that had just survived the flatbed version of the aforementioned ride, however, did not wait for an invitation to disembark. Kenworth, Peterbilt (Pete) and Freightliner poured over the area, sniffing and scouting with a genuine thankfulness to be alive and traveling of their own volition again.

Axel exuded his usual hypnotic calming presence as he held the lead rope of each animal being packed, stroking its nose, his gentle voice surrendering them captivated and still while pack saddles and half breeds were put into place. Items waiting to be packed were scattered about on the ground on top of white canvas manty tarps waiting to be wrapped, looking much like multiple little picnic sites. Sam and Brett methodically went from pile to pile, wrapping each load, pulling the tarps as tight as possible, and securing them with a long nylon rope that was eventually chain tied and secured back to itself. In favor of the speed of setting the panniers and the fact that some of the manty loads would be top packed, the hard boxes were next in succession. They would sling the others last.

Sam was tall enough to hoist the heavy panniers to the giant mule's back, but it required both hands to pull the straps over the hoops and set the buckles properly. Nobody else could even see the hoops much less reach them, so as soon as he had the load chest-level high, Brett and Kat would slip underneath and hold it up from the bottom, effectively freeing Sam's hands to secure the buckles. A quick repeat completed the first set, making it ready for cover and lashing down. Axel was almost nose to nose with Calvary as he stood with his enormous head down in willing resignation, allowing for the scratching of his long black ears. Sam and Brett made laps around them securing the load with a series of repeated knots, "tie backs," and "tuck unders" that eluded Kat's sensibilities. Without words, each knew what the other was doing next and where to be; it was like witnessing the choreography of a silent symphony.

When everything was checked, tightened, rocked and retightened, and everyone was finally mounted, Sam lightly spurred Damascus. He took the lead with his right hand grasping the lead rope setting the pack string into motion. Behind the three-and-a-half-car mule train, Axel was now having a discussion with Hazard like a parent preparing a small anxious child for a shot. Kasi-Ann followed with Kat, and then Brett, bringing up the rear.

The trail was both treacherous and beautiful. The great slides of granite rock along the mountain face were difficult to navigate at times, making the progress slow, but the fresh air was invigorating to both man and beast.

Sam's arm was already getting sore from checking up his long-legged horse to keep him from running his usual Damascus 500. He would walk a normal pack string to death as he charged forward carrying only Sam, and they were dragged along packing dead weight, but the draft-crossed mules easily bore their loads. Even the gaining altitude as they ascended higher and higher did not burden them.

They wound ever upward on what seemed like never-ending switchbacks, the riders constantly wary of the narrow path often close to the rocky edge. Multiple little springs and waterfalls sprung from the mountain side, giving them cool refreshment from their uphill toil, the sun, all the while, smiling down on them.

Things were going almost a little *too* smoothly, Sam had just begun thinking when the mule train derailed. Sam had just rounded a switchback followed by a bit of trail parallel to that of the trail below him when one of the mules decided to take a shortcut. Instead of following Damascus and the lead mule Abby, Cross spotted a shortcut and stepped out of line to jump ahead.

Along with failing to turn his blinker on while passing, his feet slipped as he landed short of the trail, and he began to slide down the side of the mountain directly into the path of the following riders below. Abby stumbled immediately as Cross's full body weight pulled her down with him. Calvary staggered as he tried to keep his feet on the rocky trail, the weight of his two siblings now adding to his load.

Having to abandon his hold on the lead rope, Sam was shouting to Kat and Kasi-Ann to get out of the way before the sliding mules crashed into them, and for Axel to try to keep the rest of the string on their feet. Hazard, however, had not finished outlining his last will and testament and would not be moved.

Kasi-Ann was trying to back up and give Sam room to come down, but Penny had nowhere to go with Kat and Delilah so close behind. As Calvary was finally overtaken, the caboose then became the Little Engine That Could. Sabbath simply decided she couldn't hold the line on her feet anymore and the little mini mule flopped down on her belly. She lay there, holding the weight of three mules two and a half times her size for just long enough for Abby to get her on her feet.

Sam had jumped off Damascus, and on foot, skidded his way down the steep slope to recover the lead rope. With extravagant effort, a half dozen prayers and small favors called in, all the mules were eventually on their feet again and their order put back to right. Sam marched them back up the trail and through the switchback, muttering.

It had all happened so quickly, there had been little time to react, but Sam had moved like lightning. One second he was above them, and the next he was right in the middle of it, threatening to go careening down the mountain with them. With less than a deep breath Sam was back in the saddle leading the procession higher once again.

Kat, fumbling through a prayer of thanksgiving in her head, caught Sam's eye as he again rode above her. He nodded. That was it. They would talk about it later. Maybe. Everyone seemed to have gotten the memo or couldn't manage words just yet either, so they rode on in a temporary reflective, grateful silence.

At last, the trail cut through the lofty pine trees spilling out onto a lush green meadow. Ahead, individual rays of sunshine were reaching down to touch on an icy blue, horseshoe-shaped, freshwater lake, twinkling a welcome.

Dismounting, everyone enjoyed a quick stretch and surveyed the area while they tethered their animals to set camp. The first order of business was to relieve the mules of their packs. Knowing what was packed in each one by its color or design, Kat and Kasi-Ann commandeered the kitchen items and unearthed the sandwiches planned for their picnic lunch upon arrival. Setting those aside, they constructed the orange pannier table and set it up by what looked like the usual tent site. There had been quite a bit more snow in the mountains the previous winter, and the summer sun had apparently caused an overgrowth of grass.

With considerable effort, Kat dragged the canvas bag housing the wall tent over and began fishing it out. Sam was already eye-balling ridge poles that would be cut for the tent frame as soon as he could lay his hands on his saw. But presently, his stomach could swear that his throat had been cut. He momentarily settled for putting everything in sensible piles, hobbling the stock so they could mill about and eat or drink as they pleased, and all but arm-wrestling Kat for a sandwich.

Under a canopy of shade, they sprawled out on the soft emerald carpet of grass, eating their simple meal. Kat hadn't noticed during the journey when Sam's contentment had arrived, especially considering the mule escapade, but she could see it enveloping him now. He lay on his back with his hands underneath his head, and his dusty, sweat-stained, signature, Gus style, palm leaf hat tipped down over his brow. For safety, a colt .45 Peacemaker hung off his right hip in an aging, tooled, brown, leather holster on his belt. He looked like a page ripped straight out of a Louis L'Amour book.

His breathing was slow and steady, but he was not asleep. He was steeping, soaking in Mother Earth, and it almost appeared that she was returning his embrace. Kat was so enthralled by the picturesque scene he cut that it took a moment before the sound of dogs barking invaded her mind far enough to find her. She snapped from her thoughts to see the three dogs barking in the direction of the lake, hackles rising off their backs like inverted icicles.

And then she saw it. A huge grizzly bear was pacing back and forth on the other side of the lake. Sam was already on his feet, pulling a Weatherby insurance policy out of his saddle scabbard.

*How many times had they talked about this? How many?!* Kat blistered the inside of her head with her own burning questions. Being in the mountains means being in bear country—everything from proper food storage, to carrying a weapon for protection, was exercised because of the probable, not possible, *probable* encounter with "Cruncher," as Sam so affectionately put it.

She shivered as the name bannered across her mind like a moving billboard. Panic was starting to take hold of her. Before she suffered a complete leave of her senses, she called out to Sam. Fear had already strangled her powers of speech, and it came out in a strained whisper.

"Shhhhhh ..." Sam gently soothed with his left hand held up to her. His right hand was already gripping the pistol, and the .300 Weatherby was already slung over his shoulder. His eyes never left the bear.

They were about 200 yards from the water's edge on their side, and the bear was on the bank of the other side, eyeing them closely. Kat didn't know how far away it actually was, but she knew how far it wasn't—and it wasn't *far enough*! She knew the bear could close that distance in a matter of seconds. The lake was barely five feet deep in any area, the bottom plainly visible.

Telling his family to stay put, Sam began walking toward the water, accompanied by the dogs. He looked fearless. His gaze darted over the herd, taking an assessment of where everything was. They too were still, very aware of the predator sizing them up.

As Sam reached the water, the bear stood up, grunting. It was clear that he was displeased to find that he had uninvited house guests making themselves at home right there in his living room. Sam's mind raced with all the possible scenarios that could play out. Still towering, the bear continued his aggression with a hair-raising snarl. Sam maintained his ground and fired a shot in the air. The bear flinched as the sound echoed off the mountain and reverberated across them.

He was thoroughly ticked off, but Sam had his attention now. Then the bear opened his mouth and clapped his teeth together sounding nearly as loud and every bit as intimidating as the gunshot. Kat winced, thinking to herself, *that's why he calls you Cruncher.*

The dogs were pacing and looking at Sam like *"All I got is a pair of deuces. I fold man,"*

Finally Sam's poker face won out. The bear reluctantly lowered himself back onto all fours and turned away, heading into the trees. Relieved, Sam breathed deeply, realizing now that he had been holding his breath for an unknown expanse of time. He knew full well that could have gone very differently and was, in truth, a bit shocked that it didn't.

He watched the bear for a long while as it ambled up the hill, away from their campsite. Sam might have talked it out of a full-on brawl, but it was by no means afraid of them, and its slow retreat said as much. Cowboys 0, Bears 0. As much as Sam liked to win, he was more than content to call it a draw.

The dogs were suddenly courageous again, firing a litany of *"And don't come back... You don't scare me..."* barking at the bear's disappearing posterior.

Sam walked back to his family and hugged a still wide-eyed, trembling Kat. The boys looked as though they might burst with pride, and their formulating renditions of the story when they got home would likely paint a comic book scene of their father single-handedly staring down a bear at arm's length with nothing more than a stick.

Kasi-Ann was speechless for the first time in her entire existence and simply clung to Kat's hand. In an effort to keep them calm, before anyone could say anything, Sam reiterated his bear "spiel" with the same attention to order and effort that a tired flight attendant gives to the preflight information at the end of the day.

He'd said it enough times. It was more than memorized; it was ingrained.

Finishing, he simply stated, "We've got work to do, let's get to it."

"Hurry up! We're burnin' daylight ..." Axel chimed in with his favorite John Wayne-quoted response to his father's orders. Kasi-Ann at last cracked a smile. Brett just rolled his eyes and started looking for the pile with the wood saw.

Kat was glad to again busy her hands with something—*anything*. It was going to take a month of Sundays to get over that particular encounter, especially knowing that she would be sleeping in Cruncher's living room tonight as well. Another shiver coursed over her along with a revamped version of The Three Bears—in which, somewhere along the way, Goldy had dyed her hair red.

It was a full family effort, cutting the poles and setting up the tent, but it was managed relatively quickly. Kasi-Ann was now busy, going about picking up the sawed off bits of poles and stacking them in what would soon be a good-sized wood pile.

Sam was methodic in his set up. It was well known to each of them what tasks were to be performed first to ensure that they would have shelter, filtered water, and the ability to cook or be warmed by a fire. That same wood pile would be the last order of business before riding out when they were finished. It was Sam's custom to leave a bit of split and stacked wood for the next inhabitant of the area.

This would more likely be a useful commodity to others in a more organized camping area than here in this remote place, but his rules of conduct were the same for any place he stayed. It would be tidied up to leave no trace, or at the minimum, restored to the order in which it was found, or better, and prepared for the next arrival. Knowing how it felt to ride into a place in the dark, frozen, and bone weary to find ready firewood, he gladly left this simple gift behind.

These mountains could deal out very harsh weather no matter the time of year, to which Sam would merely recite to himself in his weatherman voice, *"Welcome to Montana. It is what it is, and if you don't like it, wait five minutes."*

The late afternoon sun was beginning its descent, casting an orangish-pink glow across the still water of the lake. Beyond where the light touched, the green reflections of the trees played in the shadows. The surrounding dark blue mountains still bore whitecaps as they stood sentry just below the early August sunset.

Courtesy of some "Boy Scout in a Bottle," Sam had the beginnings of a roaring fire started, and Kat was rummaging through the soft-sided ice chest for their dinner. Inside the tent, a six pack of children and dogs were bouncing from one bed roll to another, effectively undoing any sense of order or tidiness Kat had achieved just moments prior, as any self-respecting youth would.

Leaving the fire to burn down and the fumes to dissipate a bit before attempting dinner, Sam absentmindedly walked down toward the water. Dodging the multiple, scattered, round stones bleached white in the sun, he thought he might be able to hop from one to the next and never have to touch the ground—a game Kasi-Ann would enjoy. His smile faded as his mind transcended further to his own childhood memories.

He knew it was coming—it always did. The tidal wave was inevitable, but the tears stinging at the corners of his eyes still surprised him. It was always a mix of emotion for him because this favorite camping spot was the one he grew up going to with his family, and it was the last place he had seen his father alive. They had been hunting in the back country, and his father had ridden out a day ahead of him. By the time Sam packed their camp out and returned home the following evening, his father had passed suddenly from a violent heart attack. His mother had followed six months later, seemingly of a broken heart.

Kat stood watching him as he stared at the sky. Uneasy thoughts began whispering to her. How could it be that such a beautiful place could make such a giant of a man look so small and vulnerable? She knew he was adrift somewhere between past and present, both happy and heart-wrenchingly sad. Kat also knew there was not a day that went by that he didn't miss his father. It seemed there would be no amount of time that would lessen the ache that surfaced in his eyes when he spoke about him. Before they married, Sam asked Kat to go with him to this place. Until she saw it, she could never have imagined the beauty or understood the connection that Sam felt to it.

He confessed that his sudden disappearance after the funeral had brought him here. He had raged in frustration and confusion at God for what seemed like hours until he collapsed in exhaustion and slept for the first time in days, right there in the grass.

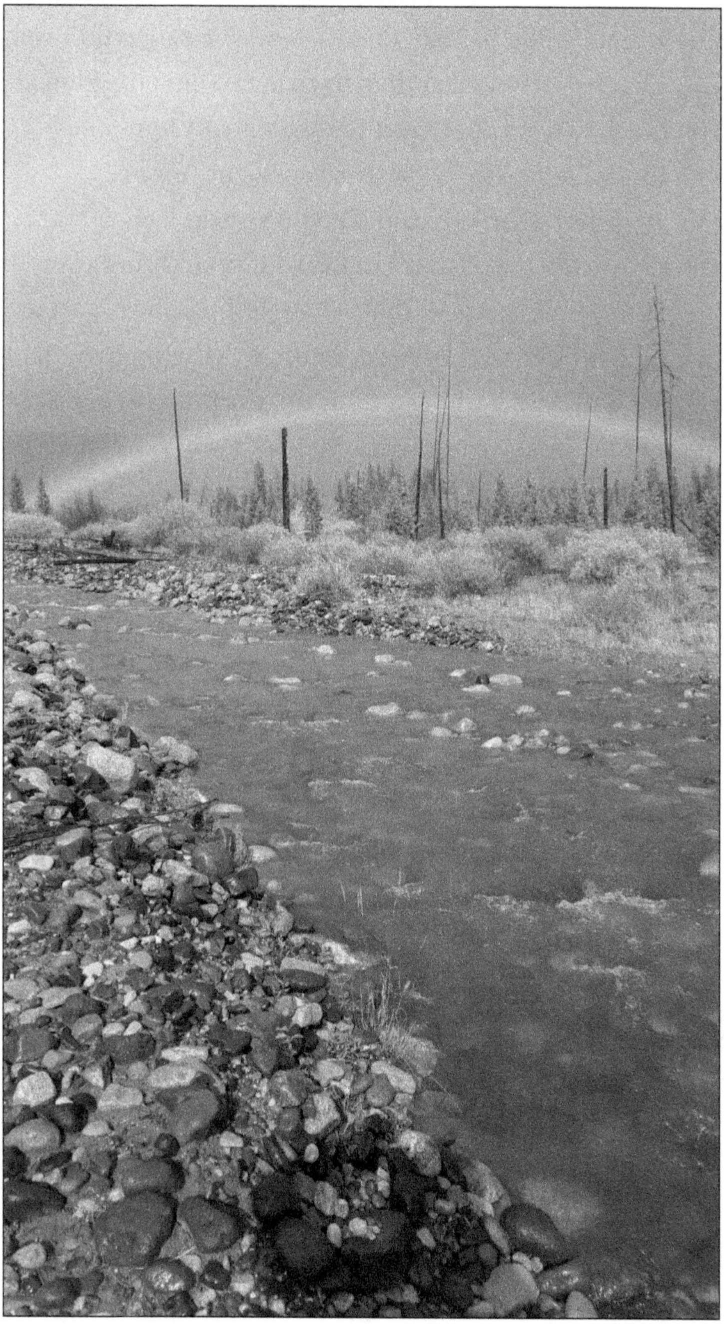

When he woke, the sun was bright and warm on his face, making it impossible to fully open his eyes. Sam could no more explain what happened next than fly to the moon on a John Deere tractor, but he swore that God had spoken to him—in his own father's voice. Or maybe it was both speaking at once?

He knew his father's voice but couldn't help feeling that it was God's words telling him that He heard him and that everything was going to be all right. With tears streaming down his face, he opened his eyes to find a brilliant rainbow hanging over the lake, though the only rain had been from the storm in his heart.

He told her that he immediately felt an unexplainable peace over his whole being and that visiting this place was the only time he could feel it—the peace that surpasses understanding. Every day it was better, but this was the only place that the enemy's voice berating him for not being there was silenced.

Sam didn't even hear Kat come up behind him; he was so lost in his own thoughts.

"Howdy, handsome, ya come here often?" Kat asked softly.

The facade of being strangers was a game they often played.

His response was not immediate.

"Oh, a couple of times a year if I can swing it," Sam half sighed and half replied, staring blankly across the lake.

Just when Kat thought the lingering silence answered her query better than he would, he continued.

"You?" he asked, turning to look at her.

Hoping the silly game would lighten his mood, she played on.

"Oh, about the same," she answered back as she picked up a small smooth stone and skipped it across the water. "I only ever come up here with my family. It's kind of a special place for us. We have lots of fond memories here."

His only reply this time was a thoughtful smile.

"If you don't have any plans for dinner I'd love to introduce you to them," Kat finished, a teasing smile twinkling in her green eyes.

Sam was suddenly all in.

"Well, ma'am, I am a married man, but supper does sound mighty appealing."

He held out his arm and Kat entwined hers as they began to walk back toward the camp.

"Besides, the odds of a man getting invited to dinner by a beautiful woman in the middle of the wilderness have to be pretty small. It's either a once in a lifetime opportunity, or a fairytale with a nasty witch in disguise—either way, mind you, I'm willing to take my chances," Sam said, unable to resist provoking her.

"I see," Kat began, suppressing a sizable giggle. "Well your bravery is duly noted," she finished with a convincing nod.

They continued arm in arm toward the tent in silence, each again lost in their own thoughts for the moment.

"You don't have any kids locked away that you're planning on fattening up or anything do ya?" Sam suddenly questioned.

Feigning shock, Kat gasped and swatted his arm.

"I'm going to tell your wife you said that! Maybe I'll get to meet her someday. I'm sure we would get along famously."

She giggled softly, thinking to herself, *"I have four children, and I'm married to the oldest one..."*

It was the best five days they could remember in a very long time. Chalked full of fishing, stone hopping, intermittent nature hikes, mule retrievals and variant forms of lounging, the days flew by like the flipping of pages in a book.

Thankfully, it was not the remade story of The Three Bears that Kat had feared. Cruncher had blessedly elected to holiday elsewhere for the weekend or was being treated for PTSD after the gunshot. Either way, he had not surfaced during the remainder of their stay.

On their final day, Sam was busy making his usual "last camp day breakfast," which amounted to whatever meats and various states of potatoes were uneaten over the course of the last few days, accompanied by a dozen eggs. All of it would eventually be buried under a mountain of shredded cheese just prior to serving.

In his rancher's opinion, anything cooked over a wood fire was going to be breathtaking, and because meat and potatoes were always involved, life didn't get much better than that. Kat was of the ranch wife's opinion, that anything she personally didn't have to cook or clean up herself was breathtaking, even if it was a peanut butter and jelly sandwich.

While breakfast came together over the fire, the Portable Patterson Hilton was torn down, bed rolls rolled up and piles of pieces and parts cropped up, waiting to be packed. The dogs were snoozing in the morning sunbeams, waiting for their turn at the cast iron pan's offering. All around them, birds chattered, and squirrels flitted from tree to tree. Nobody was in a real hurry to leave, least of all Sam. But going back to the real world was inevitable, and he knew it. He was thankful for the time they had been able to spend together and the overdue relaxation he had enjoyed.

As the last items were packed and gear checked, Sam took one last look at the now-vacant campsite. Everything appeared to be tidy and in its place. The wood pile was in a perfect little stack, and the morning's fire had been doused with water to ensure it was completely out. The only thing left to do was to say goodbye to that part of him that remained there.

He knew he would be back, but he couldn't help comparing the feeling of leaving this sanctuary to relinquishing one of his own children. As he stood surveying the scenery one last moment, a sudden breeze passed over them.

He inhaled the fresh smell of the mountains and lake, drawing them all in as though it were a tradeoff. If he had to leave a part of himself here, he was going to take a part of this place with him. Permanently logged and locked safely away in his memory bank, he could recall it at will. Whenever the trials of the real world fenced him in, he could be wild and free here. Then without another thought he effortlessly swung up into the saddle and nudged Damascus down the trail.

They were leaving early enough in the day that riding out in a different direction that would take longer was of no consequence. The trail was a much easier descent, and a more leisurely ride suited them all today. They soaked in the sun and scenery until the trail began to widen and the lower roads became visible.

When the fragrant sea of pine trees opened toward the bottom, Sam hesitated only a few seconds. He knew if he turned and looked back, he might not muster the gumption to keep going. He lightly spurred Damascus urging him forward.

A quiet resignation set in, and he could hear, *"It is what it is"* echoing in his head. He was switching to autopilot—almost a sort of a safety mechanism. When they pulled into the driveway sometime later, he realized he didn't even remember loading the horses or driving home.

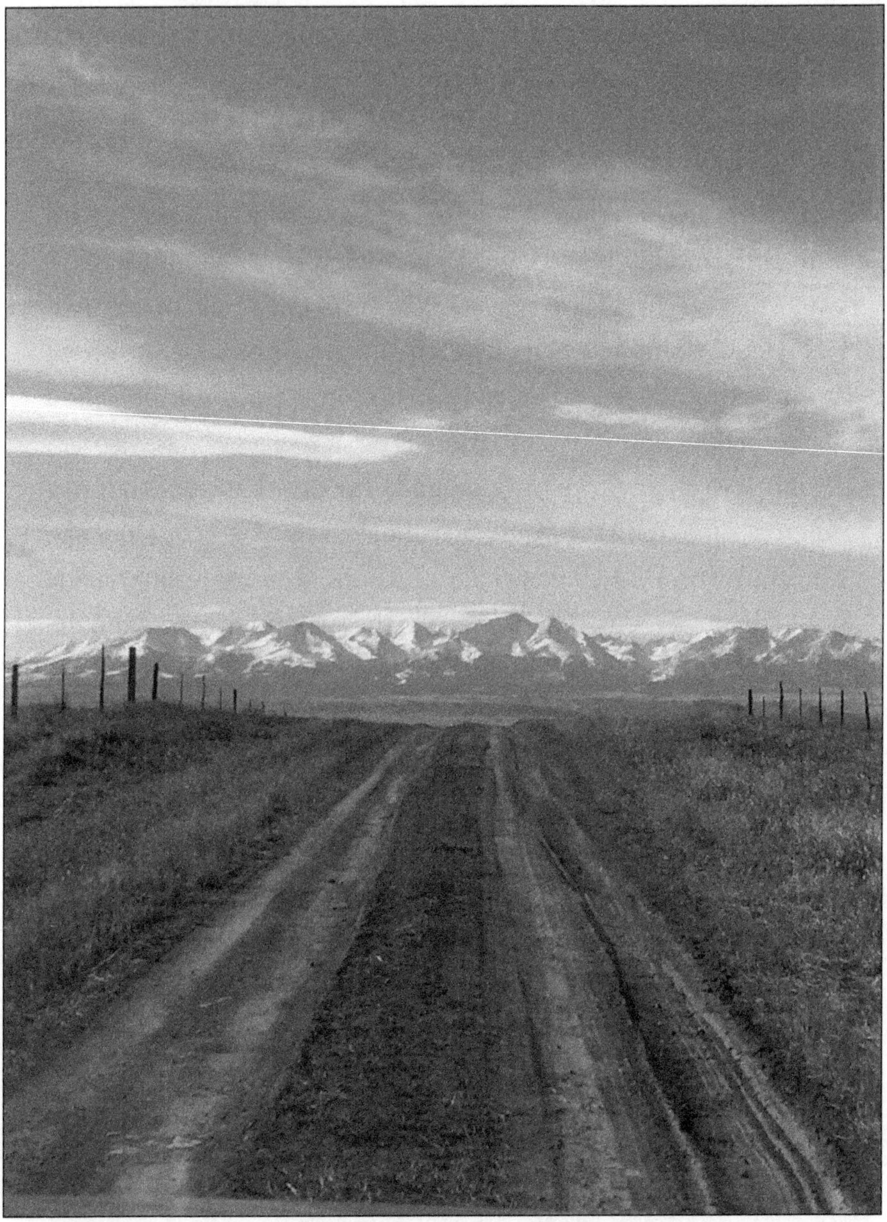

CHAPTER 7

# To Everything There Is a Season

Summer vacation was drawing to a close. Soon school would start, reordering the routine that was their daily lives to again include the schedule of the school bus and innumerable sports and clubs. Sam would add the Family Uber Driver title to his already-bursting resume, and Crankenstein would again enter stage left of Kasi-Ann's ongoing dramatic saga.

At dinner one evening, Kat mentioned that there was a message on the answering machine from her mother. Their customary visit before the school year began was scheduled for this week. Kasi-Ann erupted into a mixture of cheering and singing. She loved having her grandparents visit. Nana Posie and Papa Kenneth especially looked forward to their summer's end visit with them.

Petunia Rose might have been the name Kat's mother was given at birth, but when she met Kenny, he claimed her as his favorite Posie, and it just seemed to stick.

Kat bore her greatest similarities to her mother. Posie had an enormous personality packed into her small stature. She was the best storyteller in the whole world. She did voices and acted out several parts, more like a play than the simple telling of a story that she said lived in the wonderland of her mind. She would take the children to the park with a picnic lunch and spread a large blanket on the ground. After they had played awhile and had their lunch, they would sit on the blanket while she would spin one of her tales. Like the Pied Piper, she would draw in everyone within earshot until the blanket and grass around it was full of kids and whatever adults were with them.

The adults would inch in slowly, feeling a bit sheepish at how their younger counterparts had just joined right in, innocently as children do, but they would all be welcomed and ultimately held spellbound as Posie spoke. Each was a magnificent adventure that even Kat had admitted to being just as enraptured by as an adult as she had been a child. Perhaps even more so, as she became wise enough to appreciate the precious gift her mother possessed and shared so willingly.

Much like Kasi-Ann, as a child, Kat also suffered from night terrors. They were so vivid and real that she had a hard time going back to sleep, especially fearful that it would just start all over again. Posie would stay with her and tell her a story until she fell asleep again.

One night, she told Kat that her pillow was her dream book. If she had a bad dream, all she had to do when she woke up was turn her pillow over and she would be on a new page or maybe even a whole new story. From that day on, she never called out for her mother again. She flipped her pillow and fell asleep, confident that the next story would be a good one.

Decades later, Kat not only still employed the very same tactic, but she passed it on to Kasi-Ann. Kat had grown up without TV, but her children, unfortunately, hadn't been spared that catastrophe. She told Kasi-Ann her pillow was the remote control.

Whatever was playing in her mind that upset her would go away with the trusty flip of the pillow, because she had just changed the channel, and now it would play something happy. The only time Kat still had to go to her in the night was when she couldn't wake herself from the dream, and lay there tangled in bedding, howling to high heaven.

Papa Kenny was a much quieter soul, a genuine compliment to his beloved, he would say, since she often talked enough for both of them. He would sneak a wink at Posie to assure her he'd meant it in good humor, but oddly enough she'd have been too busy talking to have heard him.

He was kind of a practical joker and loved children, particularly teasing them. Papa Kenny had told the children from the time they were all very small that he had a mouse that lived in his left shirt pocket. His name was Whiskers, and he was in charge of Papa's money. He never kept his paper money in his jeans, but rather in the snapped shirt pocket of his western shirts. He would never wear a button shirt because it was a pain to get the button undone, but he said Whiskers liked the snaps better because they were easier to open and close.

When any of the children had a birthday, he would have Whiskers count out $1 dollar bills, one for each year since their birth to put in a birthday card for them. Nana Posie, being also a fantastic artist, would construct an elaborate homemade birthday card, and somewhere on the front you would find Whiskers wishing them a Happy Birthday. During the boys' spring and summer birthdays, he might be fishing, while Kasi-Ann's winter birthday card scene could find Whiskers sledding or skiing.

When they would go places with their grandparents and ask if they could purchase a snack or beverage, he would tell them to ask Whiskers if it was all right. Kenny would then tilt his ear down toward his left pocket to listen. If Whiskers granted them permission, they could reach into the pocket to get the money. Being the terrific tease he was, sometimes he would listen and then look at them sadly and shake his head no. They would giggle and tell Papa to ask again. Whiskers always said yes the second time, especially for a "Pretty please, with sugar on top."

During a discussion about spoiling grandchildren on their last visit, Kat declared that she had never known the Bank of Whiskers to be closed. Kenneth simply reminded her that all correspondence from non-shareholders must be submitted in writing, and with another good-humored wink, changed the subject.

The grandparents arrived three nights later as scheduled. Kasi-Ann practically wore a discernible path on the hardwood floor running back and forth from the picture window and living room where she was attempting to watch a movie to pass the time. The window faced south toward the road where they would come in from, but there was no hope of seeing the vehicle for the apple orchard. Still, she paced back and forth for nearly three hours, checking the window's tacit report every few minutes.

Finally, just when she thought she'd burst from waiting, Kat hollered, "They're here," peering out a kitchen window that faced the driveway.

They were practically mauled upon entry. After a mob of hugs, the boys brought in their bags, and they all settled into the bright blue-and-yellow patio chairs on the back porch with some lemonade.

They enjoyed the rest of the afternoon in the backyard, catching up. Kasi-Ann was content to hover her usual three feet off the ground, alternating between cartwheels, spontaneous bouts of show and tell, and every manner of bouncing. Axel was quietly working on a leather knife sheath, and Brett was trying to take a nap in the grass, but a persistent Peterbilt kept pawing him for attention. After dinner Sam suggested an evening of fishing on the Yellowstone River that coursed not more than 1000 yards from their front door.

The first full day of their stay was the beginning of the fall roundup. Sam had spent the last few days gathering leftover salt and mineral from the scattered feeders and delivering bloat blocks and good hay to the cattle in preparation for their return trip home. Even with the cattle somewhat congregating around the hay they were recently gifted with, it was going to be a couple of full days of riding to gather all of them from several sections of Montana mountain pasture. They would then trail them home to the ranch where they would occupy the lower hayfields, freshly relieved of their final cutting of hay.

Posie and Kenneth would take Kasi-Ann to town with lists as long as their arms of school supplies, clothes and groceries to buy. Kasi-Ann was excused from gathering cattle with the understanding that she was needed to help ramrod the "return-to-school roundup," and Nana Posie would likely require help keeping Papa Kenneth and Whiskers in line.

The power struggle was a quiet one, but quite real all the same. It was well known that Kenneth would declare that he wore the pants in the family, but Posie was going to tell him which leg went in first. Kasi-Ann was simply all in whenever delegated a job to do.

As their car pulled out of the drive early that morning, six riders and three dogs went through the gate and fanned out, traversing over the hill heading north. Taking a mental note of all the ground they needed to cover, Sam already had a deep seat and a faraway look. Kat was busy reminding the boys to stick together and look out for one another.

Visions of snakes, sliding off steep mountain terrain or badger holes lying in wait to break a horse's leg threatened to fill her mind. Being a Patterson ranch wife and mother had given her more experience with accidents and opportunities for treating injuries than her nursing career would ever be able to boast of.

"Oh, they'll be fine, Mother Hen," an exasperated voice from her right broke in. It was the elder of the two brothers making up the fifth and sixth riders.

Chase and Shane McCoy were as familiar with every inch of this ranch as any of the Pattersons, having been childhood friends of Sam. During various parts of the boys' toddler years, Chase had even come to live with them. Kat was convinced on more than one occasion that when she left for work each day, the children were the only adults left in the house.

"What makes you so sure I'm not talking to you two, Rip?" Kat asked smiling.

She had hung the nickname on him after one of his late nights in town when, while well-oiled with Pendleton, his mouth had been writing checks his body couldn't cash.

He was a giant of a man and a force to be reckoned with, make no mistake, but outnumbered, he was still only one man. Kat had been the voice that answered the call to retrieve him. She spent the early morning hours stitching and mending both torn flesh and clothing. Since then he had done a lifetime of growing up, but she still enjoyed poking him about it every now and again.

"No worries, Kat, I shall be my brother's keeper," Shane promised before Chase could warm to the bantering of insults. He and

Kat were both quick witted, and the prospect of a verbal sparring match always overthrew them.

Shane hadn't always walked the straightest path, either, but Sam didn't profess to have had an unblemished report card, and he had loved them like brothers all of his life. Kat was inclined to do the same, which often made them subject to her unbridled opinions, no differently than any other family member.

Naturally, Brett and Axel idolized them. They were a pair of rodeo clowns compared to Sam's all-business manner, but humor had yet to ever impede them from doing a hard day's work.

Truth be told, Kat welcomed the friendly conversation. So far, the only participation Sam had offered was hollering at Pete to "get back." The "truck trio" of four-legged hired help was meandering behind the horses. They were never to walk ahead of them, but Peterbilt tended to get sidetracked when he wasn't focused on the job. Kenworth and Freightliner kept their expected distance, likely snickering a bit at Pete for getting reprimanded.

They rode the first few miles to the pasture, catching up on all the summer events. The McCoy brothers had been as busy as everyone else in the country trying to make use of Montana's "other season." It was a standing joke that the state only had two: Winter—and road construction.

Winter could take its sweet time melting away to spring, and by the time spring arrived, summer was half over. Summer happened to be in full swing this August day, already sporting a balmy 70 degrees at 7:30 a.m. The weatherman promised a hot one with a couple subsequent scorchers on its heels, each promising to outdo the last.

As they crested the hill and approached the gate to the first section, their posse was spotted by a couple of bandit yearlings. The black, baldy pair had either gotten the memo that today began the fall roundup or were just being typical teenage brat yearlings and immediately headed for the pucker brush to hide. It was a fair assumption that the bawling taking place during their retreat was the sounding of an alarm that the cavalry was upon them.

Approaching the section gate, the horses could almost smell the game of cat and mouse afoot and began dancing in anticipation of their turn through the barrier like they were all champion roping mounts. They would have to be all of that, along with a mix of bloodhound and two parts camel over the course of the next few days.

Sam held the gate while the others filed through. Chase didn't even bother to check his horse up and wait for any instructions or plan formulating. He knew the drill. He just crammed his flat brim hat down a little tighter and lit out toward a bunch of brush off in the distance where cattle would be seeking shade from the rising hot sun. The riders quickly separated to scour the four corners, shoving cattle toward the center until a herd came together.

The dogs didn't need any orders either. They were also now in full working mode, demonstrating the same divide-and-conquer approach. They could go where horses couldn't go, helping to flush cattle out of their hiding places. With a series of hand signals, Sam could even give them instructions from great distances when they couldn't hear him.

Once a sizable group came together, the cattle could be trailed back home. It was ideal if they could all be accounted for in one trip but certainly not probable. Most of the cattle were willing to give up their positions and fall in line, especially when staring down the barrelhead of being left behind, but there will always be a few problem children inclined to swim upstream.

Today that part was being played by ol' Number 57 and her mob of brutes, numbering eight in all. Chase was riding flank toward the back third of the herd when the infamous No. 57 decided to make her play. As though she had suddenly decided she was done filing along, she squirted a hard right, breaking off from the herd, along with her would-be cohorts. Chase reacted instantly, following them into the thick timber. They had apparently rehearsed a crafty plan, all scattering in multiple directions, making it difficult for a single rider to follow with any hopes of grouping and gathering them up. It was definitely atypical cattle behavior, worthy of commendable praise, and Chase was truly a man to give due credit, but he was presently too busy swearing a blue streak about the situation to award any ribbons for bovine genius today.

Even riding point at the front of the herd, Sam had eyes in the back of his head. The instant they blew up, he knew it, but he wasn't one bit concerned. He joked in reference to their last name that the brothers were the "Real McCoys," but it was the gospel truth. He trusted their judgment and ability without question. Even if an extra hand would have been helpful, it would almost have been an insult to Chase. Sam held his position leading the herd ever onward.

Damascus, however, was not burdened by any such cowboy code of ethics. He undoubtedly wanted a crack at No. 57. He had more cow sense than any cow did, knowing what she was going to do half a breath before she did. Sam knew to just give him his head and stay in the middle when it came to those situations, and Damascus would have her where she needed to go before he could say otherwise anyway. They were twin spirits, each with their own special brand of talent and skill set—a relationship that worked because they were each willing to let the other shine in their area of expertise. And Sam knew at any moment he could be on his back with all the air in the world around him, gasping to get enough back to whisper with.

Back in the timber, Chase had his hands full, ducking tree limbs and skirting fallen logs, trying to outmaneuver the ringleader he was beginning to believe was a four-legged direct descendant of Houdini. He had tried hollering at Pete who was closest to him when the runaways bolted, but he knew that was a waste of time. If he could just get ahead of No. 57 and direct her back, the others would surely follow, but this was proving to be beyond difficult.

Looking ahead, he could see the end of the tree line, and he knew the rocky bluff on the other side would be nearly impossible to descend. Surely, she would stop and turn back at that point, or go off the other side and break her fool neck. The *"It'd serve her right"* smirk he was enjoying at that thought soon melted into an incredulous face of blinking disbelief. She charged right over the top without a second thought. To make matters worse, in their infinite wisdom, the seven lemming partners in crime came from various points in the trees and followed right behind her.

Chase inched up to the edge and peered down the rocky slope, his Palomino dancing and snorting nervously. He could see the cattle making their way toward the bottom with considerably more ease than a horse and rider would manage and turned in frustration to head back to the herd. No. 57 was amassing quite a rap sheet, and this latest stunt was by far the most animated.

As he came up behind Kat, who having lost the coin toss, was blessed with riding drag, he could see her mopping the dirt-turned-mud from her face.

"Take no prisoners, Rip?" Kat chided.

He launched into a detailed tirade, beginning with what a trashy, no-good so and so No. 57 was, and ended a fair bit later, somewhat out of breath, with "He was no man from Snowy River."

"They'll still be here tomorrow," Kat offered, but he was still too exasperated to do much more than remove some of his own sweat mud puddle with the dusty, black-and-gray paisley wild rag tied around his neck.

He hung back and rode next to Kat, neither of them talking for some time. The sun was towering high overhead, and the only breath of wind felt like a blast furnace. Finally, Chase broke the silence.

"I'm getting married," he suddenly blurted, sounding both nervous and in genuine need of forgiveness, like a first timer sucked up against the back wall of a confessional.

It had been such a long time since they had seen the brothers that Kat had no idea there was anyone applying for the position of Mrs. McCoy.

"Well, congratulations, Chase, that's wonderful news," Kat replied. "How long have you had that under your hat?" she followed.

"Two months," he answered sheepishly, staring at his saddle horn. "We haven't told anyone yet."

A few minutes later he spoke again, even more tentatively.

"I wanted to ask Sam to do the ceremony—do you think he'd do it?"

"Only one way to find out," Kat remarked. "Do we know the lucky lady?"

"No. She's not from around here. Her name is Jodeen."

Kat immediately burst into song replacing "Jolene" with Jodeen in the popular Dolly Parton hit. Chase's expression demonstrated that he had found zero humor in her play on names.

"Loosen up, Rip! Ya gotta admit that was kinda funny," Kat challenged. His brows knitted together into a face of almost anguish.

"Glory, are you that worried Sam will say no?!" she asked in genuine surprise.

His eyes were fixed on the reins he was flipping absentmindedly between the middle and ring fingers of his left hand. The dust from the herd ahead of them was swirling around their faces making it hard to see.

"No," he began quietly. I just can't imagine anyone else doing it, I guess."

It was barely audible by the time he'd finished the sentence. Kat thought to herself if Sam said no, she'd send him to heaven *today*, but ultimately it was, of course, his choice to make. For a man who could talk a solid hour, covering the merits and arguments of a particular brand of tires, Sam was, in his own opinion, "no good at speechifying."

Nothing more was said on the matter presently, as they were approaching the gate going back over the hill to the ranch. Sam had already opened it and took his place off to the side counting heads as they filed in. Once they figured out how many were gathered this round, they would know how many were left to go back and find tomorrow. He was busy making marks in his book as he counted.

It was coming on evening, but the sun was still relentless. The cattle were spreading out in the hay fields, appearing happy to be at the end of the trail at last. They were soon all jockeying for position to get a drink from the irrigation ditches.

Posie, Kenneth and Kasi-Ann had just driven in from town as well. Sam took Kat's horse to the barn to unsaddle her while Kat helped them pack everything in. They had brought supper with them, and everyone congregated on the back patio to eat. As hot as it was outside, the old ranch house was hotter still, a mere degree or two shy of Hades. The backyard at least offered some shade beneath the many massive cottonwood trees and the breeze was now much cooler. Sam sat studying his shirt pocket-sized notebook between bites. He kept all kinds of notes in this little rancher's mini bible, from calves being born and tagged, dates and numbers of cattle in specific grazing areas, to bad report card marks for troublemakers like No. 57. Ones with enough bad marks could be first numbers on the Naughty List that earned a ride to town, headed for the sale barn. He was busy pouring over how many cattle were in that section, and how many they had brought in today. According to his numbers they were only short eight. He casually mentioned this to the McCoy brothers who were intent on stuffing fried chicken and mashed potatoes in their faces like it was the last supper.

"That's pretty good," Sam said.

Considering he had previously moved several pairs from other sections until all the cattle were in one place—getting 492 of 500 in a single trip was fairly impressive.

"Probably start at daylight again tomorrow—fetch up the stragglers," Sam said thoughtfully, still staring at his book.

There was no break in the munching mouths as the McCoy brothers nodded their agreement in unison. They would stable their horses for the night, taking up residence in the spare bedroom and on the living room sofa.

The next day Sam, Chase and Shane left early to gather the remaining eight. They returned late that evening dust covered, weary and disgruntled. They had ridden every corner and hadn't seen hide nor hair of the mob now being renamed "The Hateful Eight."

The next day was the same. This time, their arms and faces bore scratches and gouges from riding every inch of the thicket and dense timber that was surely aiding and abetting the renegade cattle. It had been hot enough to fry an egg on your forehead and the men were drained from the heat and frustration of not finding the cows.

As they passed through the gate between the mountain pasture and the hayfield, they walked through all the assembled cattle brought in days before. That's when Chase saw her. It was No. 57! He had covered enough miles chasing her to recognize her backside anywhere. He took off riding to get a closer look, and sure enough, as he approached, he could clearly see the red ear tag bearing the number 57. He spun his horse and hit a full gallop heading back to Sam who was still looking on, bewildered at his sudden departure.

"Let me see that book, Patterson!" Chase bellowed before he had completely reached them again.

Sam began to fumble in his pocket. He pulled it out and handed it to Chase who snatched it up and started flipping through pages. He scanned through Sam's notes and looked up as he was doing the math in this head of the marks made as the cattle had filed through the gate the first day. They were all there. All of them! All 500 miserable, black, bald-faced cows were accounted for. Sam had just miscounted. He knew exactly where No. 57 and her cohorts hit the bottom ground and came into the rest of the herd between Sam and the other riders, completely undetected. He was instantly furious.

"They're all there—count them again!" he said and tossed the book at Sam.

Again, he spun his horse and headed straight for the barn at a high lope. He skidded to a stop out front, tethered his horse to the rail, and stormed across the drive to the house.

Shane and Sam followed a few minutes behind after Sam had rerun the numbers and confirmed Chase was indeed right. The cattle were all accounted for, and they had just ridden the hair off their horses for two consecutive days for nothing.

Chase's powder keg could lead to a fairly atomic explosion, but while his fuse was known to be short, so was the recovery time before the dust would again settle. This was about as upset as Sam had ever seen him, and justifiably so. He took his time unsaddling Damascus, and then moved on to Chase's horse. After he had all the gear taken care of and the horses brushed, he headed for the house. Chase had already finished eating and was sitting bolt upright in his high-backed log chair, staring at Kat across the table. He was still visibly angry.

Shane began fixing his plate in the kitchen, stealing a glance into the dining room where Sam was sitting down next to Kat.

"Chase … I'm sorry…" Sam began, but Chase cut him off.

"Nope, I don't want to hear it, just get in the pickup. You're driving me to town and buying me a drink big and strong enough to clear the rest of the dust I've choked down for that past two days, chasing eight ghost cattle, and that's the size of it," Chase spewed out, doing his best to keep from yelling.

He stood up abruptly.

"Kathryn, thank you for dinner. I believe I'll be on my way now," he said with a curt nod, grabbed his hat, and stomped toward the door.

Sam sighed deeply and turned to look at Kat. She simply nodded.

"I'll be back in a while," Sam said, the resignation heavy in his voice, and kissed Kat on the cheek.

He and Chase were headed back out the door as Shane sat his plate on the table and took the seat Chase had just vacated.

He smiled a giant bird-fed cat grin at her and said, "Well this is a treat—dinner *and* a show," and then started shoveling food in his mouth.

Kat just looked at him as he began eating. She was suddenly mentally exhausted. Shane's manner had always been more relaxed than his brother's. It was evident that he was mildly enjoying this new development. Kat was attempting to process everything that happened in the last ten minutes. She doubted Chase had even tasted the supper he all but inhaled before the volatile eruption that followed.

Shane took his time eating. He figured by the time he loaded the horses and met them in town, Chase would have soothed his temper with a couple doses of Pendleton and be reasonable again.

He also had the vantage point of being able to see both sides of the equation they were no doubt still busy trying to solve. Sam didn't have all the details about the eight cattle that went over the bluff; he was just going by the numbers. Chase assumed the eight stragglers not accounted for in the book were the ones he chased.

At the end of the day, it was a simple mistake of math that had resulted in two very long, sweaty and tiresome days of riding. Shane knew Sam well enough to know he would want to make things right for any mistake and would be willing to accept the verbal thrashing his brother was no doubt currently blistering him with. He winced a bit at that thought. He decided he was definitely not in any hurry and if Kat had prepared a dessert with their meal, he intended to eat it, regardless of whatever his stomach had to say about it.

It was almost 11:00 p.m. when Sam finally crawled into bed. Kat rolled over toward him and put her head on his shoulder. Sam sighed deeply, the toll the day had taken on him was evident.

"Well, that was hands down the most expensive mathematical error I have ever made in my life. I bet the guy deciding how many lifeboats would go on the Titanic didn't feel as bad as this. Okay, that might have been slightly worse come to think of it, but this is the pits!"

"Oh, Sam…" Kat whispered and gave him a squeeze. "I'm sorry this happened, but honey, nobody is perfect."

"I listened to Chase go on about it for two solid hours. By the time Shane showed up to get him, he had barely gotten started on reading me the riot act. When they finally left, I had a bill for drinks, two orders of wings, group therapy and one wedding ceremony," Sam finished sounding beyond frustrated.

Kat bit her lip stifling a giggle. "*That was clever, Rip,*" she thought to herself. There was nothing she was going to say that would be appropriate, so she let a reflective silence fall gently between them and only answered him with another squeeze. Moments later, he was sound asleep.

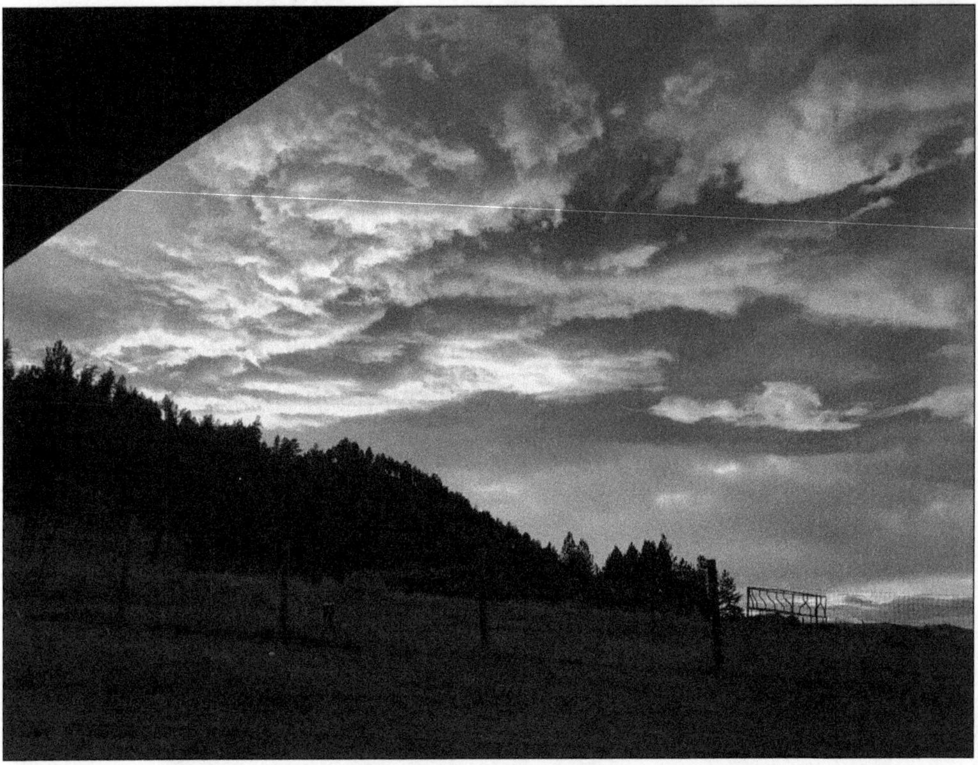

CHAPTER 8

# Our Faith Is Tried by the Fires of Affliction

The next morning, Sam woke earlier than usual. His internal alarm for 5:00 a.m. sounded about 4:10 a.m. His stomach was growling about his belly button rubbing on his spine.

As he recalled the previous night's events, it occurred to him that dinner had been the last thing on his mind. Food was the *only* thing his mind could manage just now, as he set out to gently unbury himself from the Kat bear hug he was still in. Mentally and physically exhausted, neither of them had even wiggled during the night. She was reluctant to let him go and even pouted a little in her sleep as he turned her back over onto her own side of the bed.

She would have looked at the clock and declared the time to be some manner of zero dark-thirty, or at the very least, an unholy hour of the day to be up, but she barely stirred as he pulled the covers back up over her. He smiled to himself, thinking that sawed-off little redhead even tried to boss him around in her sleep.

He bent down and kissed her forehead, put on his slippers and soundlessly closed the bedroom door behind him. While the coffee pot was brewing a pot of the finest mud west of the Yellowstone, Sam rummaged through the fridge. He found his dinner plate covered in plastic wrap on the second shelf along with a dish of berry cobbler.

"Only get one trip around, Patterson, dessert first," he thought aloud, as he grabbed the ceramic bowl and popped it into the microwave.

He knew something sweet this early in the morning was nothing but a bellyache waiting to happen, but it didn't deter him. And if it weren't for his overactive metabolism, his wife's cooking would have made him as wide as he was tall years ago.

He traded the dinner plate in for a more traditional breakfast large enough for everyone to eat by the time Kat's eyes popped open at 7:30 a.m. He heard her moving around the bedroom and handed her a cup of coffee as she entered the kitchen.

"Thank you," or something that sounded like a muffled version of it disappeared into his chest as she all but leaned on him, burying her face amid a sleepy semblance of a hug.

Clad in a fluffy, pink robe, she and her coffee were nestled in her prayer chair a moment later. She spent the first part of her day there, reading her Bible and having a bit of quiet time with the Lord. She called that quiet time "coffee for her soul," and claimed that it set the tone for her whole day. Sam's church was, in his mind, anywhere he was, most specifically in the middle of a saddle horse somewhere out in God's gym, but he obliged his wife with regular attempts of attending church because he knew it made her happy.

It was the last weekend before school started. Kat's parents would leave later this afternoon, and there were no specific plans or expectations for the day—absolutely nothing a single phone call couldn't change.

Two hours later, Sam answered the buzzing cell phone in his right shirt pocket without even opening his eyes. His oversized, chocolate brown, leather easy chair had again swallowed him alive after breakfast, and his full belly had overtaken any inclination to fight back.

He was wide awake barely a second later to the sound of a single word—FIRE. He hadn't bothered to say goodbye to the neighbor calling or return the footrest of the chair to its lowered position, he was on the move and shouting orders. The boys, recognizing the tone of their father's voice, had flown down the stairs, grabbing at hats and boots on their way out the door.

Jack Yates, a neighboring rancher, had placed the call that set them into instant motion. A welding project on an old trailer had let loose a spark and started a fire that took only a few minutes to get completely out of hand. The parched, late summer grass and usual west wind were fueling an inferno that was headed straight for them.

Sam quickly loaded a water tank onto the flatbed of the old red Ford feed pickup along with a couple shovels. They flew down the driveway heading for the mountain pasture.

A thick, black, ominous cloud of smoke was billowing in the air already. They were nearing a small tract of land that belonged to yet another neighboring ranch, situated right between the Patterson and Yates parcels. They happened to be developing an access road to the area and had a D-6 Cat dozer parked there. Sam instructed the boys to take the pickup and go back around to the other side toward Yates's fence line. He would use the Cat to doze a fire line and hopefully stop or at least delay the fire. He started the dozer and began heading downhill toward the fence. It was a considerable hill and the equipment could have used a good warming up before moving it, but there wasn't time. At the bottom of the hill, it began to sputter. It then gave a sudden lurch at the beginning ascent of the other side and stopped.

The pungent, sulphuric smell of the smoke burned his eyes and nose when he climbed out of the cab. The fire was close—much closer than Sam had anticipated. As the flames licked at the grass at the top of the hill he was just trying to climb, he quickly understood the equipment failure was a blessing. He'd have driven right into it. In the time it took to process that thought, the fire had raced down half the distance of the hill. Abandoning the dozer, Sam turned and began running back up the hill he had just descended, wondering if he could run faster scared than a hungry fire.

The heat was incredible. Sam didn't chance a look over his shoulder; he knew he was running for his life. If he stumbled or tripped, it could mean the difference between reaching the pickup where the boys were waiting with the water tank—or not. The smoke was scorching his lungs with every breath, making it even more difficult to run uphill.

When he finally made it to the top, he could see the pickup in the far distance. Thank God, they had made it all the way around already. Now he just had to get there. It seemed like an eternity that he ran, his chest heaving. Just then Sam felt the breeze in his face. The wind had shifted! He still didn't dare look behind him, but he knew this was buying him precious time.

At last, he reached the pickup and hollered for the boys to get in. They were standing there watching him running toward them, torn between staying out of reach of the fire and rushing to their father. They had taken an old coat from behind the seat and soaked it with water in case the fire had gotten any closer. Brett tossed it on the battle-scarred flatbed behind the water tank, thankful that they hadn't needed it as he dove into the passenger side of the pickup beside Axel, landing half in his lap. Sam jumped behind the wheel and floored the gas pedal, kicking up almost a rooster tail of dirt behind them.

He didn't know what to do other than to put some distance between themselves and the fire. It was futile now to try to soak the dry prairie grass at the exterior borders of the ranch. It was already breached and much bigger than one man and his water tank. In his mind, he was frantic, trying to will his thoughts to find some semblance of order. They had to go back to the house. The fire was less than two miles away now. The possibility that he may have to defend his land and home was becoming very real.

He raced down the driveway and screeched to a halt in front of an open-faced shed where the quads were parked. There wasn't time to saddle a horse. Again barking orders, he told the boys to move the grazing cattle to the farthest eastern pasture. Sam then started the White tractor and set out toward the washout pond. There was still some water there he could use.

A high-pressure pump and hose used for cleaning cattle trailers was still in place from the last washout. He quickly kicked the pump on and anchored the hose so that it would just spray out onto the grass and then proceeded north to the fence line separating the hay fields from the access to the mountain pasture.

Sam was a flawless operator. He dropped the bucket of the tractor and started ripping up the ground next to the fence. His skill made even this task of jostling over uneven ground look effortless. In very short order, he had a fire line dug two tractor bucket widths along the whole fence. When he finished, he headed back to check the water pump. He shut it off to prevent any overheating and heard the welcome sirens of the fire and brush trucks coming down the drive.

The giant red truck slid to a halt next to Sam with the fire chief's head hanging half out of the window.

"We're going to try your access road to the north, Sam—see if we can hold it off. Aerial help is on the way, but they're still an hour out."

Not waiting for a response, he slammed the truck into gear and took off again.

Kat was running down the driveway to the shop. "Sam, I called Chase and Shane; they are on their way. What are we going to do with the cattle? We have to get them out of here!"

"I know, honey, I know," he said, trying to be calm for both of them. "Go start my truck, and call…"

His ringing cell phone cut him off. It was Lars Amdahl, another rancher in the next town over. The news was traveling as fast as the fire. The short conversation answered their question. He had a large pasture with good water about twenty miles away that wasn't being used that they could immediately take the cattle to.

Both men were a bit hard of hearing and used to talking quite loudly, so Kat was already abreast of the entire conversation before Sam even got off the phone. She took off down the drive and jumped into the pearly maroon-and-white 900L Kenworth and started it up.

Sam nicknamed it "Half Painted" because it was dark maroon at the bottom and faded steadily all the way to the middle of the truck where it eventually became white, making it look like they had only painted the bottom. Kat sat for a moment, marveling.

For a vehicle that did one of the dirtiest jobs on the planet, it was immaculate inside, but that had always been Sam's way.

She inhaled the earthy tones of black cherry and leather, recalling the first time she had ridden in the truck with him. It seemed like a lifetime ago. Snapping back to the present, she chastised herself for frolicking down memory lane with a genuine crisis at hand and jumped down to go find out what the rest of the plan was.

In that amount of time, Sam had caught up with the boys and told them to push all the cattle to the corrals and talked to Chase who would be driving the other truck as soon as they arrived, which appeared to be presently.

The deafening Hank Williams Jr. music preceded the black Ford pickup kicking up dust in the drive by a full minute. Both front doors flew open simultaneously and the McCoy brothers were in motion.

"Stephen is on his way with his truck too, I just got off the phone with him," Chase hollered at Sam as he jumped in the baby blue and white 900B model Kenworth parked across from the shop, fresh from yesterday's washout.

Shane was getting instructions on where the portable loading chute was. A second later he took off across the hay field to go get it with the hydrobed on Ol' Red and bring it to the corrals. Sam's long legs scaled the aluminum stairs into Half Painted in nearly a single step and headed for the corrals as well.

Brett was seamlessly weaving through the maze of corrals, opening the gates to make room for all of the cattle to come in at once while Axel held them captive in the corner of the pasture nearest to the entrance. The smoke in the air was getting stronger. The cattle stayed put, bunched in their corner the same way they would prepare to weather out a storm until Axel heard Bret hollering to bring them in.

The boys were closing the entrance gate behind the last of the cattle filing into the corral as the portable loading chute was put into place, and Sam began backing Half Painted up to it. Brett began shuttling groups of cattle toward the truck. Everyone seemed on board with getting loaded and the heck out of Dodge. Mothers and calves almost clung to one another in the frenzy, making the gathering of pairs miraculously simple. No hot shots were necessary or any excess hollering or shoving—they all seemed to have gotten the memo that this was not a drill.

There was no evacuation protocol, but to Sam there was only one way to load cattle, and that was to do it once and do it right. He added numbers in his head as he moved mothers and calves to their respective places.

Even loaded heavily enough to make a DOT officer sweat, it would take each of the three trucks two loads to ferry all the cattle to safety. Time was of the essence. Brett and Axel were scurrying back and forth, moving cattle into groups, and holding them in different sections of the corrals until they could be loaded. Dust and smoke mingling together made the air stagnant.

By the time they loaded the second round of cattle, air support was finally visible to the north, but it was still going to be a long night of babysitting flying sparks and debris.

Sometime around 2:00 a.m., Sam finally sent the boys to the house. He and the McCoy brothers were split up along the perimeter of the hay field nearest to the gate of the mountain pasture. As much as the sight of an open gate grated Sam, he knew the cattle were all safely removed, and the fire truck that arrived early that afternoon was yet to return through it. He also knew that the closing of that metal gate was not a barrier against the fire, but his mind fought against its opened status as though it might.

Not knowing what was happening up there, how quickly they were getting the fire under control, or not, was forever bludgeoning his thoughts. The desire to go charging up there to help or at least assess the situation for himself was almost overwhelming, but he knew he couldn't leave.

Just through the opposite gate, on the other side of the pasture, was the stack yard with hundreds of tons of new hay in the form of round bales that were freshly stacked, mushroom style. When Kat had brought them out coffee a couple of hours earlier, she noticed a random spark loose in the breeze had found its way to a single round bale by the gate that had not yet been shoved up to the rest of the stack.

Chase didn't wait to see what damage, if any, would come of it; he simply grabbed the tractor and pushed it out of the stack yard and toward the irrigation ditch just beyond the washout. A few feet shy of the ditch the bale burst fully into flames and then a cloud of white billowing smoke as he raised and tilted the bucket downward plunging the bale into the ditch and dousing it with water. It still took a fair bit of bucketing and splashing water on the large bale to put it out. The executive decision had undoubtedly saved the Pattersons hundreds of thousands of dollars in hay, never mind what other damages they might have incurred if the hay fire had spread to the other outbuildings and barns. Portable water tanks and weed sprayers filled with water had been loaded onto Ol' Red and the 4-wheelers, and they were continuously traversing back and forth over the property, chasing sparks and drenching small fires.

Kat was either pacing the kitchen, forever looking out the window toward the pasture, or pacing the driveway in between, supplying the men with food, drink and encouragement to keep up their energy.

Her instinct to bake in the face of adversity had been a learned behavior placed in her from the time she was a child. If a family had suffered an illness or injury, or heaven forbid, some type of tragedy, her mother went to work in the kitchen, trying to keep her hands and her mind busy. First a casserole, then some homemade bread, followed by some kind of dessert and heaven only knew what in the end. She would say in times of trouble, she had a need to knead, and she welcomed the comfort of working the dough. When she finished, she would single-handedly deliver a week's worth of food to the family in need and stay to see what else she could do to be of service to them, likely including a thorough kitchen scrubbing and freezer defrosting.

Her mother also had an odd tendency to pray aloud while she worked, though it sounded much like a conversation in which she both asked questions and tried to answer them in the next breath. Posie spoke to God like she spoke to a best friend, so there were no fancy words, just her heartfelt concerns poured out for anyone within earshot to hear.

Amid her pacing, Kat had just dismissed the looming thought of defrosting her own freezer when Shane emerged through the mudroom screen door. He looked beat. He pulled the scarf down from his mouth and nose, leaving a line where the dirt and smoke stopped halfway across his face. His dark eyes were barely visible among the grime and black circles of exhaustion encompassing them.

"We're going to start taking shifts so we can each get a little rest," he said, sitting down on the wooden bench that surrounded the perimeter of the mudroom except for the doorway.

Above him, old horseshoes all welded together had been nailed up for coat hooks, lining the wall in the same manner, bearing jackets and hats of every size and variety hanging from them. He groaned as he bent over to remove his dusty, worn Olathe boots and slid them under the bench in line with the rest that were residing there. The tall leather tops were so seasoned that they fell over sideways opposite one another, looking like the lop ears of a faded lime green bunny.

"Of course," Kat replied. "The spare bedroom is already made up."

Shane nodded and mumbled a barely audible thank you over his shoulder as he headed down the long hallway to the spare bed he had spent nearly as much time in as his own.

Kat looked up at the kitchen clock. Dawn had crept in at some point while she was pacing. Leaning on the kitchen counter, she gazed out the window into the morning sky, straining to see the crimson sunrise behind the black-and-gray smoke attempting to blot them from view. The house felt stuffy, but there was no way she was opening any windows or doors with all the smoke in the air. Just being out there for the length of time it had taken to deliver the last round of sandwiches and coffee to the men had made her eyes burn.

She had returned a short time later with some worn-out old wild rags they could tie around their faces to keep from breathing so much smoke. She went from having three cowboy firefighters to three train robbers in the space of about two minutes. At least that was about the length of time it took the McCoy brothers to each wolf down two sandwiches and a half a pot of coffee.

With full stomachs, they were happy to tie on the faded scarves and be about their business, which amounted to finding yet another opportunity to chide Sam about his ghost cattle or some other escapade they had all been on together. Heaven knew there had been plenty.

She wanted to fast forward to some future happy time when they were all together, and they could at last look back on this event and be able to smile and laugh about their antics, knowing they had successfully navigated past it. At this point, there was still too much that was up in the air, and still too much potential for being "up in smoke."

"No!" she suddenly said aloud. "Kathryn Ann, we are not going to start thinking like that. Lord, please guard my mind and my mouth, I refuse to be ensnared by my own words ..." she prayed purposefully out loud with new determination on her way to the shelf, housing her prized Betty Crocker cookbook.

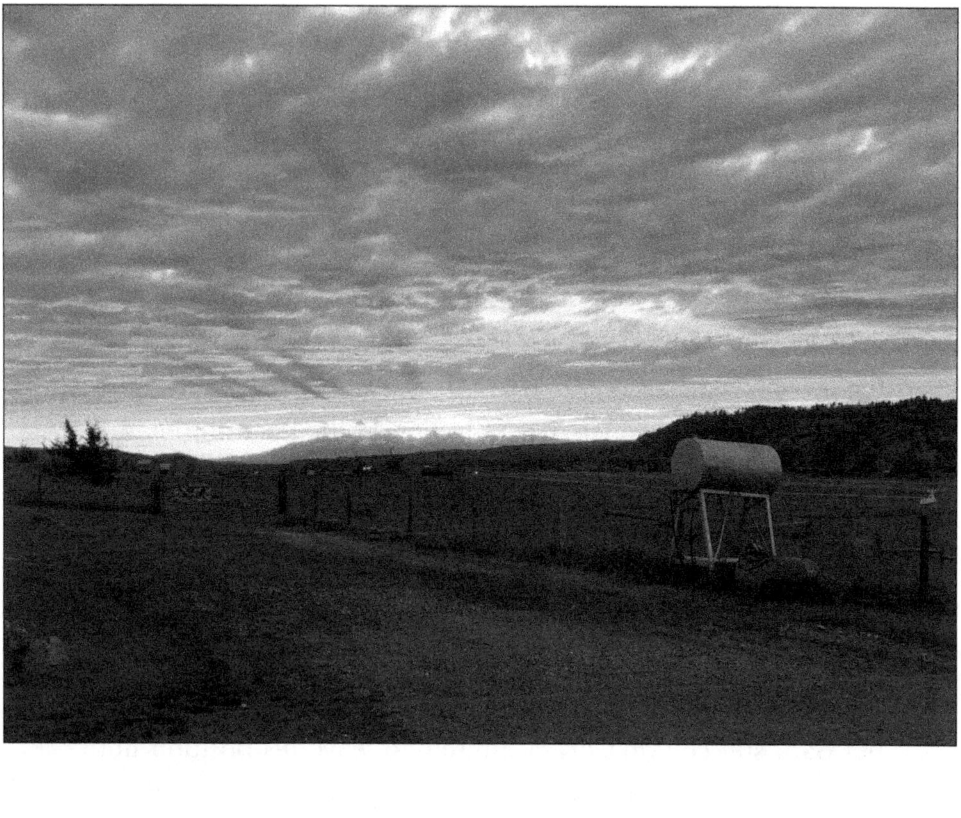

## CHAPTER 9

# Beauty for Ashes

Sam sat staring blankly into space at the long dining room table. The morning sun of three long days since the fire started was beginning to come up, sending individual beams of light peeking through the picture window, stealing their way across the polished oak surface to where he was sitting hunched over an untouched cup of coffee. His reflection in the light on the table held a haunted face, smudged black with ash and dirt. His hair was disheveled, and he was a week overdue for a shave. He still had not been to bed, despite Kat's pleading for him to get some rest. The McCoy brothers hadn't been gone a full hour.

The rainstorm that had blown in the night before had finally turned the tide and helped put the fire the rest of the way out, but Sam still couldn't bring himself to leave his position until now. Thankfully there hadn't been any lightning that could have brought the potential for more trouble instead of relief. Puddles had formed everywhere, evident of the abundance of rain that had been sent in answer to their prayers.

Kat stood in the kitchen, trying to make a breakfast that none of them could stand the thought of eating. She couldn't help thinking about the number of times she had heard her mother use the expression that something needed "a good cleansing fire." She had said it herself in reference to her own messy kitchen, or on occasion of her recipe book collection that had grown out of control, spilling out of the beautiful antique bookcase that graced her dining room wall and onto multiple shelves. It implied that it would be easier to just start over with a clean slate than to try to wade through the monumental mess or attempt to put it to any sense of order. While it certainly wouldn't be the most popular choice, it was still a choice. There hadn't been any options here. The fire had chosen them.

As she turned the flame off under the immense cast iron skillet, she noticed Sam out of the corner of her eye. He was now sound asleep, crumpled in exhaustion over the table. She didn't have the heart to try to wake him just yet, but felt torn between allowing him to get a kink in his neck from the awful position in which he landed and letting him sleep just long enough to be able to reason with him about going to bed in earnest.

Everyone had assembled for breakfast and simply passed plates and dishes around Sam as they ate. Occasionally he would mumble something that sounded like he was still trying to delegate orders to Shane and Chase to fight the fire, but his eyes had remained closed. Kat knew he would be like this for several hours until his body could somehow get the message to his mind that all efforts had ceased, and he could at last be still and rest.

She seized the opportunity to escort him to bed when he suddenly awoke with a great start, clambering to his feet, shouting for somebody to close the gate. For a second, Kat had to fight back an outburst of laughter, pondering the fact that the rancher's greatest nightmare would definitely be an open, unattended gate. He had just spent the last three days straight, running wide open, ferrying cattle, fighting fire and exhaustion but the frightening image to pull him from this involuntary coma was an ajar Powder River gate. It was the first smile she had worn in three days' as well.

Moments later, she had him stripped of his soot-covered clothing and less than gracefully tucked into bed. She would wash everything later. For now, he was going to sleep, even if it meant she had to station herself at his bedside with a Louisville slugger to ensure he stayed there.

Posie and Kenneth had delayed their trip home a day or two, helping to keep an eye on Kasi-Ann who only wanted to help fight the fire, not hear about how she was too little and would only be in the way. She was currently sitting on the couch with Papa Kenneth half reading a book to Whiskers and half complaining about not having been able to help hold the fire hose. Utilizing his superpower of skillful redirection, he helped her to finish the story and decide what other things that she *could* do to be helpful.

They made a list on Kat's "chore board" from the kitchen which amounted to a dry erase board that had been framed with some old, discarded barn wood. The wooden frame had "*CHORE BOARD*" burned into it at the top and a length of barbed wire fastened to the back to make a semicircle hoop-style hanger. On the right side of the frame Sam had screwed a small piece of metal with a washer welded to it to hold the marker. It was just the right size for it to fit inside the hole of the washer without slipping all the way through when the cap was on.

On either side of the words were two livestock brands. One was Sam's and the other was Kat's. It was a homemade Christmas gift that Sam had made for her years prior. She adored his handiwork and talent, along with his ability to always produce something that was functional and practical.

It was the primary residence of her "list of lists" and a place where she would write reminders for herself of things she needed to do. She had also used it to put up daily chores for the children when they were younger and needed help remembering their responsibilities. It was currently full of chores Kasi-Ann would be busy doing, trying to do her part to help. She agreed with Papa Kenny that any chores she could do for her mother right now would be the most helpful since she was going to need a rest later too. They shared a giggle that at least she might not fall asleep at the table.

The first item on the list was to run the dishwasher. While her mother and grandparents lingered at the dining room table, she made a lap around asking each of them if they were done with their coffee cup or glass from breakfast and escorted them to a nearly full dishwasher.

Kat had been too preoccupied with getting Sam into bed before he collapsed in a heap en route that she was just now getting around to thinking about clearing away the breakfast dishes. Kasi-Ann patted her hand and told her in her best mothering voice to just sit and rest while she took care of it. Mildly suspicious and shooting her father a cocked eyebrow glance, Kat admitted to herself she was happy to just be still for the moment.

Her questioning glance was not unnoticed and when Kasi-Ann had her back turned headed for the dishwasher, he quietly pointed out the to-do list painstakingly written in her hand. The chore board was now in the corner of the spacious dining room, propped up against the wall not far from where Kat was sitting.

Posie, on the other hand, was still on about the time a prairie fire had nearly overtaken her home on her family's ranch as a child. As usual, she had gone on despite Kasi-Ann's polite interruption and the fact that neither of the other two parties were listening any longer. Kat absentmindedly noted it was nearing the end where her grandmother had taken Posie and her other small siblings down to the corrals and placed them in the large round galvanized horse trough when the fire was getting dangerously close. She had soaked a large blanket in the cold water and covered the top of it to shield them from the smoke as they huddled down inside the trough in a foot of water with nowhere else to go.

Grandmother Elliott, a determined and often sour-faced Scottish woman, had repeatedly chanted a prayer, praying a hedge of protection around them, all the while holding Posie's youngest brother who was just a tiny baby tightly in her arms. In between reciting her fervent prayer, she had told the children they were playing a game of hide and seek with the fire and if they stayed in the water, under the blanket, it would not be able to find them.

Some of the children were sitting down with water up to their little chests. She had been home alone with all six of their children while her husband was off helping to fight the fire. They had only one vehicle, so she and the children were essentially trapped there, miles from town and any neighbors. She had stood watching from an upstairs bedroom window as a wall of fire ate up acres of prairie grass, moving fast, seemingly ever-intent on their location. Looking down at the corral below the house, her eyes fixed on the water trough. It was all she could think of to do to try to withstand the flames. She grabbed the blanket off the bed and all the children and headed for the barnyard.

Blessedly, at the last minute, the wind had shifted and sent the blaze away from them. It had left miles of black, charred ground nearly all around them, right up to about 500 feet of them, but it did not claim their home or barn, or pose them any further threat. Their father had driven like a madman when he learned the fire had crossed over to Cherry Ridge where his own ranch was. He had fallen to his knees weeping and hugging them all when he returned home to find them all alive and untouched.

Kat's thoughts drifted between her own recent fire experience and her mother's chilling story. It was one she had heard countless times growing up, but until today she could not really imagine the real fear of facing down this volatile enemy. Neither she nor her children had been trapped directly in the path of the fire. Knowing Sam and the boys had been closer to it was enough to cause her stomach to give an involuntary lurch.

She closed her eyes, trying to force the image out of her mind. Her hand flew to her forehead and she took a slow deep breath, suddenly grateful that she had only picked at her breakfast. She had been too busy watching Sam to be sure he didn't slip out of his chair and onto the floor to get much of her breakfast past her lips.

Kasi-Ann had completed the kitchen clean up, started the dishwasher and grabbed the bucket of scraps and vegetable peelings that could be taken out to the chickens. She lifted the latch on the gate and stepped inside calling to them as she began scattering their breakfast on the ground inside their run.

During the summer months she would catch grasshoppers by the handfuls and deliver them as a tasty snack. They would go wild chasing down this welcomed delicacy. Before Pete's arrival, they had been able to leave the chicken yard gate open and let them free graze on their own, but for a loveable idiot, he was a known chicken hater.

After a few feather-flying, dead-chicken episodes, Sam decided to hide out in the barn next door and watch to see who the culprit was. That single afternoon's worth of watching implicated Pete as the guilty party. As the chicken involved that day had survived, he couldn't use the tried and true method of strapping the dead bird around his neck to rot where he couldn't get away from it, so he had decided to invest in a shock collar. If he couldn't be taught to respect all life on the ranch, he would not be allowed to stay. After the arrival of the collar, Pete was fitted for his electronic enhancement. At first he appeared to be rather proud of his newly acquired accessory. He may or may not have chuckled somewhat smugly at Freightliner and Kenworth that they were still wearing their old collars, which were beginning to show some definite signs of ranch wear and tear.

Sam gave him some basic training with commands and the warning buzzer and a light shock treatment in response to unwanted behaviors. Sam soon retreated again to his hideout to watch the coop.

As Pete looked around both ways, deciding for himself that nobody was outside, he started making his way toward the chickens. At halfway across the driveway, Sam gave him the warning buzzer. Pete stopped dead in his tracks and looked around again. There still was not a sign of anyone walking around, so he took another step forward. Nothing. Another step later, still nothing happened. Content in his mathematical determination of putting two and two together and coming up with five, he figured out Sam had always been there when things happened with his new collar—and Sam was nowhere in sight.

He marched right up to the chicken-wire fence and stuck his nose up to it deciding on who was going to be his bird of choice today when the devil himself sent the very fires of hell streaking through him from his eyelashes to the tip of his tail. It sent him into fits of shivers and contortions he never dreamed his body was physically capable of. It would stop for a split second, but before he could gather his wits to run, it would start all over again. At one point, he swore he could see the chickens laughing and pointing at him and the new fear that they now controlled the collar took hold. He yelped a full-detailed confession when the next bolt of lightning coursed through him, somersaulting him into the chicken fence and then back onto his feet. At this juncture, it appeared that the chickens had actually all stopped to watch. They stood with beaks agape, heads all curiously cocked to the same side.

Shortly after the thorough execution of his finale, which included a triple salchow and face-flattening landing, there was an apparent ceasefire. He lay still except for the gasping his lungs had called for in response to his less-than-graceful dismount from the collar-imposed floor routine. Pete, however, wasn't going to wait for a round of applause or another jolt from the collar. He jumped up and took off hobbling as fast as his numb and tingling paws could carry him.

He went straight back across the driveway to the dog pen, slinking in red-eyed and guilt-ridden. His fur stood up in odd tufts everywhere, and there were bits of gravel, twigs and leaves stuck to him, courtesy of his recent break dance performance. He looked as though he had barely survived a deal gone wrong needed to support a questionable habit, or at the very least, the remnant shell after a ten-day bender.

Kenworth and Freightliner eyed him suspiciously as he retreated to the confines of his own personal doghouse in the growing heat of the morning sun. He wasn't so smug today, sporting his fancy collar. In fact, his expression bore more of an air of "dead men tell no tales" and they doubted very much they really wanted to know the full story. The pen gate was open all day for them to come and go as usual, but Pete did not elect to venture outside for anything else that day.

Sam later confessed he was overthrown by a fit of uncontrollable laughter likely exhibiting some similar flailing and wallowing about that he didn't return to the house for a full ten minutes either. Pete, however, was from that moment on, officially chicken broke.

Kasi-Ann was nearly finished spreading out the chicken buffet when their often-troublesome rooster decided to have a go at her. She successfully dodged him a couple of times, but the last effort caused her to step on one of the fluffy-footed Brahma hens who gave her a verbal berating for her trouble.

Having her own feathers now sufficiently ruffled, Kasi-Ann had soon had about all she was going to take from this bully. She had seen her older brothers football punt him across the run with their Muck Boots when he came pecking at their legs, but she didn't really want to hurt him—she just wanted him to stop. The next time he came at her she slammed her overturned 5-gallon bucket down on top of him, then turned around and sat on top of it. He charged the walls and pecked at the hard sides of the bucket, but it wouldn't budge with her perched on top. She sat there several minutes talking to the other chickens that were busy tending to their haul and paying her little mind. She figured they were able to have a nice quiet breakfast without this brat of an unruly rooster bullying everyone. It served him right to have a little timeout to think about what he had done.

She made a face and nodded her head in affirmation at that particular thought and gave him another five minutes penance just for good measure. At the end of the time, she got off the bucket, dropped the chicken door and exited the gate to go collect the eggs. The bucket remained quiet with the rooster still captive underneath. She emerged again with her pockets and turned-up shirt tail full of eggs and then reached in and grabbed the bucket, finally liberating the offending rooster. She finished with a gentle scolding that she didn't want to have to tell him again to play nice and headed back to the house to wash eggs and check the chicken chores off the chore board.

It was late that afternoon when Sam finally woke up. He remembered dreaming several things, but the true content of the dreams was exiting the tangible brink of his consciousness and fading into a blurry background. What he did know for sure was that it hadn't been pleasant.

His body ached from head to toe and his throat burned with a smoke-induced dryness that even a tall glass of iced tea wasn't going to quench, but it was the ever-present thought his mind was focused on as he hypnotically went through the motions of getting dressed and headed for the kitchen. He felt like a zombie and figured he didn't look much different.

*"You look like you've been rode hard and put up wet..."* his father would have said. He could still hear his voice as plain as day despite the many years that had transpired since his passing.

He sat down in the same chocolate brown easy chair that he had bolted from at the onset of the fire fiasco days before, feeling an odd sense of deja vu. His mind quickly dismissed that, suddenly flooded by a violent recap of the fire events parading through his mind. He hadn't forgotten that it had happened, but he was still surprised by the intensity the reality of it all had just body slammed him with.

Immediately, he knew what the deja vu feeling was. It was the same way the loss of either of his parents would sneak up out of the blue and pommel him like it was the first time he had received the news. It was like being punched in the gut unexpectedly and sitting there in a ball trying to get your air and your wits back at the same time.

He sat with his eyes closed a long while, trying to untangle his jumbled thoughts. He still needed to go assess the mountain pasture, but the elusive answers to those burning questions were going to have to wait a couple days. He'd already figured that about a third of the 12,000 acres burned were within their borders. They were not the only people the fire had affected and he knew full well his neighbors were facing down some of the same game-changing challenges.

He had received so many phone calls and random friends and neighbors showing up out of the blue to lend a hand. There was so much to be thankful for, but all at once the realization of what was lost became almost overwhelming. He was the third generation to run cattle on this ranch, and as of this moment, it was drastically compromised. He guessed at the miles of fence line lost and the cost to replace each mile, shuddering at the almost $60,000 price tag his very basic calculations produced.

Sam was tugged out of his torturous thoughts of the damage by a cheerful humming. Kasi-Ann was still busy checking off her chore list, currently tidying up the family room. She had a habit of humming when she was busy with something, seemingly regardless of what it was. She might be painting or drawing, but whatever the task, she was more likely to be humming a sweet little tune than not. She would stop on occasion as she thoughtfully studied or looked over her project, then the minute she resumed, so did her humming. It was her autopilot. It was when the humming stopped that great murals in crayon miraculously appeared on bathroom walls and fingernail polish Picasso paintings emerged from the sides of dressers, so Kat had learned to absentmindedly listen for the humming that generally meant, all is well.

Kasi-Ann was so focused on her work that she hadn't even noticed he was there.

"Sorry, Dad. Did I wake you up?" she asked, her humming now abruptly halted.

"No, you didn't, sis; I wasn't sleeping. I was just checking my eyelids for holes," he finished forcing a small grin.

When he would fall asleep in the chair in the evening, she would wake him up and tell him he should just go to bed if he was tired. He would tease her and say he wasn't sleeping, telling her he was investigating his eyes looking for holes. She would always laugh and ask him if he had found any yet. The answer was always no, but he was going to go back and check some more, just to be sure.

Once when she was about three, she had fallen asleep on his chest as they sat in the chair. Sam was guaranteed to be asleep in five minutes if he sat still anywhere, so they were both napping in the oversized chair before long. She was the one who woke up first and he woke up to her flipping his eyelids open, wanting to know if he had found any holes yet.

"Whatcha up to, kiddo?" Sam asked inquisitively, suddenly feeling like he hadn't seen his daughter in weeks.

"Oh, I'm helping Mom clean, so she doesn't have so much to do," she answered back, her gaze still intent on the coffee table she was dusting.

"Well, that's very helpful of you. Thank you for doing that, honey. I bet Mom really appreciates that," he praised.

Her face lit up like a beacon.

"Yep! She's already thanked me three times! I have a whole list on her chore board and I am checking them off as I go," she finished proudly.

"That's perfect; good for you!"

She straightened the large rectangular blanket draped over the back of the couch and ran off to check her family room cleaning off the list. Sam sat staring at the blanket. It was a gift Kat had given him to cover up with in his chair. Most of the time he was too warm, but when the notion struck him to grab a blanket, it was right there waiting for him. It was a photo blanket she had made for him from an old picture of his brand burned into a wooden cabinet in the shop. The O Bar Triangle brand had been his from the time he was Axel's age and had bought his first calf. The close-up photo had been so vivid that it made the rough wood grain of the cabinet look as though it would give you a sliver if you touched it. The deep, uneven burn marks told the tale of a scorching-hot branding iron rocking back and forth in its grooves, until a satisfactorily deep, complete, black brand had been achieved.

A brand. The ranch and his brand were as much his identity as what was plastered on his own birth certificate. He was known far and wide by his name, his truck, his brand and certainly his cattle. It never ceased to amaze Kat when they drove down the road that he knew so many different trucks and trailers and who was pulling what for whom. They couldn't even get on an airplane and travel far from people and places they knew without running into people Sam knew.

It was always the same story, they would be walking along talking and someone would come up saying, "Sam Patterson, well I'll be …" or "It's been forever, Sam, how have you been?"

Sam never forgot a face, or the potential half a dozen mischievous stories he may or may not wish to have told, but Kat knew inside of five minutes' conversation when he couldn't remember the person's name. She would listen to the conversation and wait patiently for an introduction that often did not materialize. Most days she took pity on him and made a small joke of her husband's lack of manners and would introduce herself to the person, thereby gaining their name so they *both* knew who they were banging down memory lane with. But every once in a while, the little redheaded devil that sat on her left shoulder would whisper in her ear, and she would remain quiet, all the while glancing back and forth at an increasingly uncomfortable and fidgeting Sam, who knew he was going to have to confess his sin before much longer.

As always, he was a very good sport and would genuinely apologize profusely for having drawn a blank with their name. It would only turn out to be one of the many laughs they would share with their temporary company. Later he would even the score with a cold glass of water invasion to a perfectly relaxing hot shower, or simply holding her down and tickling her senseless, depending on the severity of her offense.

The meaning of "later" was a loose calculation as well. It could be later that day, that week, this century. Suffice it to say he did enjoy planning his payback and he wasn't above involving small children if necessary. Kat would know it was coming and be stepping carefully around corners for weeks expecting to be ambushed at any minute, only to find he wasn't there. He'd give her enough time to let her guard down and then scare the stuffing out of her. She'd scream loud enough to make the angels bust a harp string and nearly jump clean out of her own skin. By the time she retracted her claws and came down from the ceiling, he was waiting there to catch her.

The episode generally ended with Sam's "Gotcha …" sometimes in unison with whatever child had been hired as an accomplice to pull off that particular shenanigan.

Kasi-Ann was coming back through the living room on her way to the back patio to water the flower beds, this time with Kat on her heels. Kat noticed Sam sitting in the chair looking thoughtful and went to sit on the arm of the chair.

"I didn't realize you were up. How are you feeling?"

"Like I've been run over by a Mac truck," Sam replied, his voice still hoarse and rough from all the smoke.

"I'm sorry, love. Are you hungry? You kind of slept through breakfast," Kat teased. "Okay, *on* breakfast," she couldn't resist adding.

"I'm starving. I feel like a spring bear coming out of hibernation, but I'm afraid I've been too bone lazy to go make anything yet," Sam confessed.

"Mmm, your chair swallowed you again, didn't it?"

"Maybe …"

He looked up at her, his blue eyes regaining some of their usual twinkle. Even with amusement in his eyes, he looked weary. She had always loved that he was an old soul, but he looked like he had somehow aged from this event. It wasn't that he had gained any lines on his face or gray hair, though she expected she would be responsible for every gray hair on his head eventually. It was as though his eyes could tell a tale of time and distance. He had suddenly gained much of each of them in the short passing of a few days.

"Well, mister, let's find you something to eat; a fella your size has to stay fed up pretty regular if he's to keep on keepin' on," Kat said with a wide grin.

She was coining a phrase he had said to her while they were dating when they had gone fishing for the afternoon and his pickup broke down. By the time evening rolled around, he was remarking on how he was withering away to a mere shadow. She mentioned if he had been a better fisherman, they could have eaten some fresh trout, further rubbing a little salt in his wounds, but as it was, they would simply have to eat the apples and beef jerky she had brought along in her backpack.

He had looked at her like she was both a thief and a savior simultaneously at the late offering of her provisions. She told him that his mother had tipped her off to bring snacks along for day trips because he was always too busy to eat lunch and when delays kept him from supper, he had a tendency to get a little ill tempered.

Sam laughed at her reminder of his typical behavior as he followed her into the kitchen. She pulled the refrigerator's stainless double doors open wide and it was stacked from top to bottom with blue glass Pyrex casserole dishes and Tupperware containers of every shape and size. There were at least three desserts, one of which was his favorite—peach pie.

It suddenly occurred to him that she had been under duress these past days too. Of course, she had. Nothing escaped her notice. She had known they would be going without sleep and kept them well supplied with every manner of comfort she could scrape up for them. She herself was up most of those days and nights, feeding them, their guests and waking up Chase and Shane for shifts every three or four hours around the clock. When she wasn't seeing to their needs, she had been cooking, and if he knew her, pacing, watching, listening and waiting with them. She was here, but she shared the same fear, the same feelings of helplessness. She had even baked him a peach pie, either in the wee morning hours, or suffered the heat of the day with the oven going to give him his favorite treat.

Kat stood aside to let Sam's eyes shop the contents of the refrigerator. He stood there a long moment and then reached up and closed both doors. Then he turned, reached for her, pulled her into him and wrapped his arms around her. She was almost stiff with what seemed like surprise at first, but it only took a couple seconds before the wall came tumbling down and she buried her face in his chest and broke down crying. What remained of her bravado had melted away, leaving her vulnerable and exposed, with no choice but to feel everything she had been trying to put on a shelf to deal with after the danger had finally passed.

Every time she took down a cookbook, she placed her worry there for later so she could press on in the now. They hadn't had time to talk about it yet, and right now there were just no words. There was nowhere to hide any longer from the realization that their lives were going to change immensely. They had survived a fire without the loss of lives, any major buildings, or their home, but a cattle ranch without fences does not run cows. It would mean selling the herd Sam had worked his entire life to amass to pay for rebuilding the fences. They could have fences, but no cows, and fences don't generate income. They would either have cows or fences, but not both again for a very, very long time.

In her head, thoughts of not knowing what they were going to do were thundering back and forth like a violent storm, hitting one side and ricocheting to the other. She wanted him to tell her everything was going to be okay, that he had a plan. He always had a plan. He said nothing, hugging her tighter. His silence was deafening.

She hadn't had any idea when they had slipped to the floor, but when she finally opened her eyes, wiping tears away, she found herself in Sam's lap smack in the middle of the kitchen floor. It was such a shock she couldn't do anything but laugh. Laughter through tears was her favorite emotion anyway, so she just kept on laughing.

She looked at Sam and noticed the tears welled up in his own eyes and quit immediately. She reached up, putting her hands on either side of his face. Suddenly, she knew she needed to be the one to speak strength back into him, even if she was going to have to just call it all out in faith for the time being.

"We're going to be fine. Sure, this is going to be a major change. We'll all be making some pretty big adjustments, but Sam, we're going to walk through this together, no different than anything else we've ever faced. When God closes a door, He opens a window, and sometimes He flat doesn't give us a choice about making some changes in our lives, but He can work everything out for our good. Sometimes He even uses the trouble to push us into better things we wouldn't choose for ourselves because we want to stay where we are and just be comfortable. Every time we have to stretch a little, we are better off for it. We learn and we grow in the tough times. They have a special way of developing our character and helping to refine us."

She leaned back against his chest and continued her sermon another ten full minutes, and Sam was happy to just listen. At first, he felt a little bit bad that he wasn't comforting her and making her feel more confident about the situation, but her words were a healing balm that he was now allowing to cover him, and he hadn't realized how badly he had needed them.

He had felt like his throat had gotten tight and he could barely breathe. His chest ached reminiscently like it had during his sprint while running from the fire. His mind was a mess of a million thoughts all screaming at once, and his mouth refused to open. He was not above crying, but it was as though his emotions were completely trapped on the inside. As he focused on the sound of her crying, he lifted her into his arms and eased himself down to the floor, feeling like his entire body would give way any second. He sat there rocking back and forth until he no longer felt her trembling.

Then, out of nowhere, she was laughing. It sounded like she was laughing from a far distance, steadily coming ever closer. Then as she spoke, he saw his own body begin to visibly relax. His arms had been tense around her, though he was careful not to squeeze her too tightly. His shoulders relaxed and then his chest, making his breath finally come and go quietly in an easy, rhythmic cadence. Her voice was almost hypnotic. He pondered for a moment that this might be the reason she could talk him into just about anything. The truth of it was that the woman could sell ice cubes to Eskimos, he at last qualified.

"Sam, are you listening?"

"Yes, love, I'm listening," he lied, giving her a gentle squeeze.

"Thank you," he continued. "I needed to hear that. I know we will find our way, we always do, but I guess I needed to be reminded today."

"Honey, we have each other, so nobody has to be the strong one all the time," Kat whispered.

"I know," he answered, kissing the top of her head.

Neither of them said anything for a moment, and a quiet comfortable silence settled on them. Finally, Sam spoke.

"And if you're willing to give up the pulpit for a moment, I think I'd like to take another look in that refrigerator."

"Of course!" Kat answered jumping off his lap.

She stuck out her hand to help him up, marveling a little at how far he had to go up from the floor. He gave her one more little hug of thanks then began rummaging through the funeral-worthy spread that was currently residing in their Kenmore refrigerator.

He pulled everything out and scattered it out along the kitchen counter to get a better look at it all. In truth, he had full intentions of trying *everything*. Before long, the clanging of dishes and delicious smells coming from the kitchen had rounded up the entire household, so they all decided on an early dinner together.

One and a half plates of casseroles and salads and two pieces of peach pie later, Sam was again installed in his man-eating chair, fighting off the urge to check the underside of his eyelids for holes again. That battle was soon lost.

Everyone had congregated in the family room after supper and Kat was enjoying one last evening visiting with her parents. They would leave tomorrow now that the proverbial dust had settled.

Tomorrow was also the first day of school again, but with all the commotion in the last few days, Kat hardly felt prepared. At this moment, she hardly cared. It was nice to just be still and enjoy the blessings in front of her. The world would continue to turn no matter what, but she was choosing to step off the merry-go-round and be present. The kitchen counter was still covered in casserole dishes and pans waiting to be put away again, but they would have to do just exactly that—wait. She watched Kasi-Ann sitting next to her grandfather, playing cards. It sounded like Whiskers was cheating again, the rascal. The boys were half watching an episode of Duck Dynasty and half watching to see if Whiskers was hiding the ace of spades in Papa's shirt pocket again.

Kat was half listening to her mother and half pondering that her collective ensemble of a half-burned cattle ranch, psychotic horses, PTSD dogs and colorful family would probably qualify as the Dork Dynasty. They could probably even do a spin-off show and never be at a loss for material with all the odd happenings that they considered "the usual everyday life" around here. More often than not, the family laughed at themselves, telling others the tales of their ranch excursions, saying you couldn't even make this stuff up.

She had been threatening to write a book for years about her time in the medical field and as a Montana ranch wife—to include comparison notes of Sam's own personal clinical history. His methods of clean up and treatment, or lack thereof, would definitely lend some twists and humor to the text. For example, his cowboy version of "take two aspirin and call me in the morning" was "rub some Copenhagen in it and it'll be fine."

Sam had single-handedly extended Chris Ledoux's list of Copenhagen applications by over half again, taking credit most specifically for extensive research in the areas of worming dogs and cavity prevention.

Kat's thoughts drifted back to her mother's story. Realizing she had also heard this one as well, she didn't feel quite as bad for not giving her undivided attention just then but settled in to focus on the part that was just around the corner. She loved this story and reached for the television remote from Sam's chair arm to turn the volume down and hear it better. The boys were now listening as well.

Whiskers, having apparently been recently arrested, branded a card shark and carted off by Sheriff Papa, asked for a postponement of the card game. Everything grew still under the sound of Posie's voice. So, the piper piped them all deep into the world that was her vivid imagination and they willingly followed, without ever looking back.

CHAPTER 10

# The Great Montana Sheep Drive

The first week of school came and went in the blink of an eye, bringing August to a screeching halt and giving way to September. All attention was now diverted from the recent fire and focused on the Labor Day weekend festivities.

That Sunday marked the annual Sheep Drive. It was an event the town had concocted in answer to the Great Montana Centennial Cattle Drive that was taking place that same day in September of 1989. The centennial cattle drive was held to commemorate the 100th birthday of the Treasure state and actually took place over three days beginning in Roundup, Montana, ending in Billings, Montana on September 6th. That day began what put Reed Point, Montana, on the map, creating an atmosphere that drew over 10,000 people to watch several hundred sheep gleefully ushered down their four-block Main Street. It grew into an annual fundraiser that helped to support the local fire department, library, school and multiple town improvements.

Each year, like being queen for a day, the little, one-horse town transformed into a booming metropolis with food and multiple merchandise vendors lining the streets from daylight to dusk. It was hard to imagine looking at it any other day of the year, but the town would be bursting at the seams with people from all over Montana, neighboring states, even drawing international viewers. Similar to one of Posie's stories, it was like waking up in a magical new world that would later somehow melt away as the bell tolled, and the day was done.

But while it lasted, there was something for everyone. A car and semi-truck show put some of the most beautiful and unique machines on wheels on display for viewing and voting. They were later included in a full main drag parade of everything from horseback riders bearing flags, or a full marching color guard, floats, 4-wheelers, motorcycles and tractors. The end of the parade featured the proud local volunteer firemen and women in freshly washed fire and brush trucks with full sirens and lights blazing. If it was particularly hot and the fire chief was feeling especially mischievous, the crowd might find themselves refreshed with a random blast from the fire hose.

The family event boasted bouncy houses and face-painting stations courtesy of the resident church and a homemade pie and ice cream booth manned by the school staff. Other local organizations, clubs and individuals represented would be found in different booths, scattered along the street and intermingled among every kind of food truck imaginable.

At the north end of the street, in front of the Waterhole Saloon, an old Wild West shootout would take place, missing only the sign from the OK Corral as a backdrop for authenticity. Music and entertainment would crop up everywhere as people made laps back and forth over Main Street, never seeing the same thing twice. Then as the log-sawing contests of the afternoon faded into evening, the big band of the night would be setting up for the annual Sheep Drive dance.

As a young man, Sam had been present for the planning of the first Sheep Drive, and he hadn't missed a single one that followed. It was more like a family reunion for the families of the area because everyone who had moved away, or come and gone from town, was beckoned home to share in the fun again. The locals who helped put everything in place for the event would work tirelessly for days in preparation, finally enjoying a well-deserved evening together on Saturday before the street would become unrecognizable and abuzz with visitors.

The Pattersons were up early, making stock ready for the parade that was to begin at noon. Given the excitement, everyone was out of bed without being called and out in the main barn, saddling horses they had caught the night before and stabled in a small holding corral just beyond the barn's back doors. Brett, Axel and Kasi-Ann would be at the front of the parade, carrying the colors through today on horseback, followed by Sam and Kat in a shire-drawn buckboard wagon. Sam borrowed a favorite pair of enormous shire horses that he often drove for an older gentleman to pull the wagon in place of the mules because of their experience with people and crowds. Sheep Drive was not the place to teach massive animals manners. Mistakes would simply not be permissible, so he was calling up the big guns, literally. They were parade veterans, majestic, and impressive to behold.

This, of course, wasn't always the case. Sam already had a handful of big adventures with these two under his belt, one of which nearly cost him the very barn they were standing in. Everything ended up being big with them, whether it was an epic failure, or a great big victory, you were going to have a large time.

## The Great Montana Sheep Drive

The day had started out business as usual, hitching the two of them up for a routine driving session, but things always have a way of taking a hard left U-turn where there's no right on red on the Patterson place.

Sam had just backed them out from in front of the central barn and taken a left down between it and an open-faced shed, on a little trail that led out to the hay fields. Not being a lot different from driving a semi and needing forty acres to turn it around, Sam preferred to have ample open ground to work with when it came to the shires. They hadn't made it ten paces when one looked at the other, never mind the blinders on the headstall and apparently said, *"I don't feel like going, do you?"* *"Nope"* must have been the instant replay because they did an immediate about face, took hold of the bits and practically ran the flatbed wagon right out from underneath him.

They retraced their own steps right back to the hitching rail, but not bothering to stop out front, they picked up speed and went for broke right up over the foot-high step, headed straight through the middle of the barn.

Deciding this was as good of a time as any to consider heeding their mother's advice about joy riding, the boys bailed off just inside the door, turning the runaway trio into an uno. On the right, the back wheels of the wagon caught the edge of an old freezer used to store grain and cake in, sending it tush over tea kettle, eventually scattering its contents into the next county. As a result of that speed bump, the wagon careened into a small stack of straw bales that practically exploded on impact, filling the air with dust and straw behind Sam who was now standing in the seat, leaning fully back, pulling on the lines with all his strength trying to whoa them up.

Straw stuck to him everywhere the sweat had been dripping, giving him the appearance of having been tarred and feathered. By now, Sam had a king-sized mad on as well. It was a sheer miracle that he didn't just spontaneously combust on the spot. The shires had no intention of stopping, however and kept on running toward the double doors at the other end of the barn. As they hit them, the wagon came to a thundering halt two-thirds of the way through the barn, now wedged and tongueless. Sam finally let go of the lines and watched them run right through the doors that only the upper half was open for. The barn was suddenly much better ventilated and essentially doorless.

The pair had come quite a long way since then. Sam still got a little hot under the collar every time he thought about that incident and had no bones about verbally berating them for tearing up his barn. They even seemed to hang their heads and stare at the ground a little like they weren't particularly proud of their behavior when it got brought up.

Kasi-Ann would be taking her first run at riding a horse by herself through the parade today. She was absolutely thrilled that she got to go up front with the boys. This did not, for one minute, mean thrilled beyond words, as according to her brothers, she hadn't closed her mouth once this morning since her eyes popped open. She would ride in the middle between Brett and the American flag, and Axel who would carry the Montana flag. Her horse was also a parade-worthy alumnus. Today she would be riding her late grandfather's horse Solomon.

He acted as though he already knew where they were going. He stood taller and at full attention, ready for duty as he received his brushing and was saddled up.

The shires were dancing in anticipation as Sam and Kat made laps from front to back harnessing them. It had taken several minutes to straighten the harnesses out to even begin, and Sam was just warming to the prospect of telling off whoever had put them away in a heap instead of hanging them up properly. The twisted mess of straps and buckles was finally separated and untangled so it could be fitted over each of the horses.

This was always a bit out of Kat's wheelhouse, much like securing pack-string loads, but she did her best to be more of an assistant than a warm body that ended up in the way. Even Sam had to stretch as he placed the hames up over their massive heads and then Kat helped pull the harness down their backs and over their sizable posteriors that she was barely standing eye level with. She often joked they should have a limbo contest underneath the leggy creatures, but in truth was more worried about the two-ton middle crashing in on the party to have entertained the idea with any genuine intent.

They finally got everything loaded in the trailer and still had to drive several miles to town. Upon arrival, they would have to get everything out of the trailer, hitch the team to the wagon, cinch up saddles on the other horses and get into place for the parade at the other end of town. They had unloaded the wagon and stashed it in the driveway of a friend right at the edge of town, so they had a place to park as well as room to work with the team and the wagon.

Cars were already parked along the interstate, backed up from the exit almost half a mile. It was yet another good turnout. They were able to come into town from the back side and access the driveway from an alleyway, thus avoiding the crowd. The street was closed to traffic at the end of that first block, so people entered from there on foot. It looked like it was elbow to elbow the entire length of the street already. The food smells were so tantalizing that Kat's stomach grumbled the moment her feet hit the graveled drive, and her nose met with the scrumptious breeze floating about. She hoped her favorite Chinese vendor had attended again this year.

It was like looking forward to the food at the county fair without the prospect of a gut-wrenching ride that threatened to spin it right back out of your stomach if your timing wasn't well thought out. They did their best to frequent one favorite vendor and one newcomer every year, to wish them a welcome to the event and support their choice to attend.

Kat had looked at her watch that read 11:50 a.m. as they had pulled into the drive and was just now remembering the time crunch as she tried to silence her growling stomach with a quick gulp of water. Sam and the boys were already leading horses out of the trailer.

The three saddle horses were tied to one side of the trailer and the shires on the other where the wagon was sitting. Bridle and lead rope exchanges were flying, and Kat held the team at the head as Sam connected the tugs to the wagon. As he fed the crossed lines to the wagon, Sam hollered for Kat to get aboard and hold them still while he ran a quick check on everything.

Once he finished there, he headed over to cinch up Kasi-Ann's saddle on Solomon.

"Hey, old man," he said softly as he approached him from behind.

"Yeah, you know what this is all about, don't you? he asked, patting his shoulder. "Alright, no funny business with my best girl here, deal?" he questioned with one last downward tug on the stirrup.

With everything in order, he grabbed Kasi-Ann and plopped her on top of Solomon. She landed with a giggle and took up her reins. The boys had just grabbed their flags and mounted as well, stuffing the wooden poles into the boot on their outside foot.

"Get up," Sam said with a gentle rap of the reins and eased the team out of the drive and onto Main Street. The shires were more than ready to step out.

People everywhere were already stopping to stare. The shires were truly breathtaking, but Kat presumed it might have a little bit to do with a cowboy in a sleeveless hot pink brushpopper shirt driving a team and wagon. Heaven knew it made her heart skip a beat here and there.

It was 12:05 p.m. as they rounded the corner at the post office and turned down the next street parallel to the parade route. They worked their way to the front, passing all the other parade entries already assembled. Nancy Underwood was shaking her head from her position at the helm, saying something about how she had expected some typical "Patterson Time" today. She knew they were coming and held everything off until they arrived.

Everyone seemed to know they would be late and had some sort of comment to share. Sam didn't say a word; he just grinned from ear to ear and pulled the team to a stop in place behind his flag-bearing children at the front, just in time for "The Voice," signaled by Nancy, to announce the parade was about to begin.

As they pulled around the corner heading south through town, the same emcee that had presided over the event since its beginning was now announcing his family presenting the colors, and in her usual humorous way, commenting on the color choice of Sam's shirt as they rolled by. Without missing a beat, she moved on to introduce the shires who were in now full parade mode, prancing with heads high.

The sun was warm on their faces and shoulders, bordering on burning Kat's fair skin. In her haste, she had forgotten to apply any sunscreen. She was thankful the parade would be short and focused her attention to waving at the crowd and tossing their haul of candy gathered for the event. She knew there was sunscreen this time of year in every vehicle they owned, and even if that failed to produce, the small gas station convenience store would likely have some as well.

She took in the view of both sides of the street as they ambled by, taking note of her favorite food vendor truck while simultaneously having her interest sparked by the first newcomer she spotted. The canary yellow truck was advertising "Cheesecake on a Stick" in bold blue letters. Cheesecake, being without a shadow of a doubt her favorite dessert, she was ecstatic to meet them and give what she was sure would be a wonderful treat a thorough sampling.

After the parade, they pulled back into the driveway where their pickup and horse trailer sat with lead ropes and other miscellaneous gear somewhat askew, making their hasty departure evident. Sam and Kat quickly unhitched the team and relieved them of their harnesses. He immediately hung them inside the nose of the trailer to prevent any tangling; wishing to avoid a repeat of this morning's performance the next time the tack was utilized. They tied all the horses to the side of the trailer for the time being so they could go get a closer look at all that Main Street had to offer this year.

The first stop would be at the pie booth to deliver Kat's two freshly baked apple pies, courtesy of the bounty crop provided by their orchard this year. Kasi-Ann was bent for election to make it to the bouncy houses but attempted to wait patiently while her mother was talking with her teachers as she handed over the pies.

Kat was quick to redirect the conversation away from the topic of the fire they brought up, intent on enjoying the day, so she quickly remarked on all of the items at the booth. The table looked like a major bakery chain had just delivered a load of its finest products from exquisite pies, pastries and cinnamon rolls.

She cringed a bit at her own two pie crusts in comparison. It was a given that if she had to take her baking handiwork anywhere, it would either taste great or look great, but never both. Her pie crusts, regrettably, either ended up thin enough to read the newspaper through, or thick enough to use as a mud flap, never in between, much less perfect. She settled for knowing that the flavor of the recipe had turned out brilliantly, having sampled a little of the excess pie filling and crust remnants that she fashioned into a small turnover, barely giving it time to cool from the oven before popping it into her mouth.

Whipped cream and vanilla ice cream were being kept cold in coolers under the tables in the shade for those wishing to go all out with the already decadent desserts. With cheesecake on her mind, and Kasi-Ann tugging at her hand, she bid the teachers and her mediocre pies farewell, and progressed down the street.

They passed several booths that had clothing and jewelry of all kinds for sale. Another had paintings and rustic artwork. She marveled at the talent and creativity people had for taking what others might see as junk or scrap metal and building such interesting things out of it.

Midway down the street, there was an open grassy lot where the inflatable bouncy houses were set up. Kasi-Ann could hardly contain herself as she stood in line to buy her tickets. She had already run into a group of her friends and classmates who shared her enthusiasm, and they were practically bouncing up and down without the benefit of the trampoline as they waited for their turn.

Sam and Kat decided to visit the lemonade stand directly across the street and get a refreshing drink where they could escape to the shade of its awning and still keep an eye on their daughter. The sun was out in full force, and Kat again remembered with a frown that she was still yet to apply sunscreen. A lot of weight her nursing advice would carry on Tuesday morning if she showed up to work burned to a crisp, she thought to herself, as she watched Kasi-Ann pulling off her boots in preparation for her long-awaited crack at bouncing.

Sam was already engaged in conversation with three people Kat didn't know, so she decided to take pity on Sam and wait around to see who needed introductions to whom before she went back to the pickup for her tube of sunscreen. After the hurried nature of the whole morning, she was content to just be still for a moment and sip her lemonade.

She watched Kasi-Ann who was bouncing so high she would have bounced clean out if the structure hadn't had a roof. Her agile little body easily did forward and backward flips between the time she achieved lift off from the springy surface, until her feet touched down again. It made Kat's stomach roll every time.

Kat was, by God's own design, built low to the ground, but He had made her a devout coward of heights with a strong aversion to non-uprightness to ensure that she stay there. The simple act of witnessing either one made her physically ill, but Kasi-Ann, much to her dismay, was fearless. She would go on the Ferris wheel and other horrific rides by herself during the fair. It was all her mother could do to stand there and wait for her, eyes covered or diverted the entire time to stave off full cardiac arrest.

Behind them, in the back portion of the lot, a round bale had been set up for the bale-rolling competition. "*Only in Montana,*" Kat had thought when she first heard about the game, but she figured if medical teams could have gurney races, she had no room for snickering at the rolling of a round bale in a field for entertainment.

Marks were made with spray paint in the grass, designating the start where the bale was and the finish line the bale had to be rolled past. There was a nominal entry fee for each trio of teammates and the top three best times would actually earn cash prizes. This year's bale, however, appeared to be flat on at least two sides, causing a person to wonder if there had been some twine tension issues on the baler, or if this particular bale was simply a Sheep Drive veteran itself. Either way, it would produce a considerable challenge to keep it in motion with any less power than a freight train.

Trains were yet another unexpected treat during Sheep Drive, as the train tracks are situated literally just at the end of Main Street. In recent years, conversations had taken place, asking the railroad to relay to their conductors that they could lay off the horn a little while passing directly in front of the town's festivities—all two blocks of it. Since the formal request was made, one could easily bet dollars to donuts that there would be triple the amount of trains on tap for that particular Sunday of the year with each of the drivers competing in their own contest with the others to make their presence known to the crowd.

The Voice's updates on the doings would disappear from the loudspeaker under the tedious four standard "God Bless the Queeeeeeeen" blasts that were delivered *that* day with a lingering, in no kind of hurry, southern accent. If they had truly been trying to be annoying, they were apparently too dimwitted to slow the train down, and the drawn-out "Queen" portion ended up for their benefit only, in the middle of nowhere, between Reed Point and the next neighboring town twenty miles away in either direction.

This year, a newly adopted Sheep Drive practice included the doubling of the sheep guard. The warm bodies utilized to help haze the sheep down the middle of the street, attempting to contain them therein, would be increased at the end of the last block where a ninety-degree left turn is required to circle them back away from the crowd to their mode of transportation.

There is apparently a very real danger that the sheep could become mesmerized by the flashing light bars of the railroad crossing and run straight for the tracks before they could regain their senses. Most animals would run straight in the opposite direction of a loud and flashing unknown, but clearly, one must never underestimate the shared intellect of a body of sheep.

After all, some smarter members of the frequent-flyer sheep herds performing the event had figured out that there were multiple small children with every manner of corn dog, ice cream and french fry delights stationed among the crowd filling up the entire length of the street. Imagine the surprise of a youth caught up in watching the official commemorative running of the sheep, only to find out one has stopped and taken the liberty of consuming two thirds of their lunch before bleating a full-mouthed "sucker" and dashing off, quickly blending in among the rest.

Given that this is a family event and ghastly sheep behavior should never be tolerated, these herds have obviously been moved on to other pastures, or simply not invited back. No doubt the offending rakes are still bragging of their accolades to their grand-lambs in hushed and reverent tones. Of course, the devoted Reed

Point Community Club was in no way deterred and pressed forward, seeking a more upstanding herd, as the show must still go on.

Kasi-Ann came running up to her mother, puffing from her three trips through, a total of twenty minutes of bouncing, less one half minute recon mission's worth of finding her missing left boot, buried in a pile of youth footwear the size of a tractor tire.

The sun had begun to shift, leaving less shade under the lemonade stand awning where Kat was standing. It was now favoring the area where other customers had formed a rather lengthy line, waiting to enjoy their own cool beverage as well. Sam had been tanned golden brown from the minute the sun peeked out on April first, never giving the sun a single thought. Kat, on the other hand, was practically part vampire, cringing and making unfavorable hissing noises in response to strong direct sunlight.

There was nothing for it, she was simply going to have to go on a recon mission of her own and gather up the sunscreen. She and Kasi-Ann headed for the pickup, leaving Sam to visit, feeling rather certain he would be in the exact same spot when they returned—next Tuesday.

After the virtual outdoor sun block bath and a check on the stock, they headed back down the street. Kasi-Ann spotted their friend "Aunt Nancy" from church at the face-painting booth and asked if she could have hers done. The older woman was Kat's friend Nancy's aunt and namesake. Ever since she had come to live with Nancy's parents, Kat had adopted her as her aunt as well. She was a total spitfire, immediately beginning to tease Kasi-Ann about chasing boys and half a dozen other things while she transformed her little face into a beautiful blue-and-white butterfly.

She was a hoot in church, as you never knew what might fly out of her mouth at any given moment. She loved giving the pastor a hard time, though all in good fun. She had been a military drill sergeant in her day, and there was little doubt that she was an all-business, get-the-job-done leader, as well as a terrific smart alec. Her kindness and love, however, were still the first attributes people recognized.

Sam was, as expected, riveted in the exact same location as the girls made their way back down the street. Kat managed to politely interrupt long enough to convince Sam they should go get lunch and then get the horses home and close to water on such a hot day. There was plenty of day left to enjoy the rest of the festivities. The boys showed up right on cue at the out-loud mention of food as they made their way to their favorite establishments.

Kat and Kasi-Ann were having Chinese while Sam and the boys were having pulled pork and brisket sandwiches courtesy of a local BBQ outfit. Everything smelled delicious. Kat was hungry enough to try all of them, but contentedly enjoyed her annual favorite.

They got their food and congregated to the porch of a friend's home on central Main Street. It was the home base right in the middle of everything for several families for the day and provided a shaded place to kick back in a lawn chair in between events. All the kids knew to come back to this place and wait if they couldn't find their parents, and usually someone was there at any given time to lend assistance if a specific parent was not required. It was also the provision of two bathrooms the rest of the world wasn't in competition for, and in Kat's opinion, worth its weight in gold.

It was also located right next to a small park where music was being played by several different groups on a flatbed trailer stage during the day and several picnic tables were set up in the grass for the public to come sit and eat or listen. People brought chairs and set blankets on the ground everywhere, most taking advantage of the shade the park's few cottonwood trees offered.

The Voice was currently broadcasting the upcoming sheep-shearing demonstration and Wild West shootout that would take place at the northern end of the street soon. People were everywhere milling around, investigating the individual booths, catching up with people not seen in a long time and enjoying the music, food and atmosphere.

Kat's other good friend Carrie was just coming up onto the porch, also packing a to-go box from the famed Chinese distributor. The nearest decent Chinese restaurant was over sixty miles away and eating out was simply not something the Patterson's subscribed to very often, so this truly was a treat. The next least likely occurrence to the opportunity of eating out was the prospect that a rancher would consent to a Chinese food restaurant when the first occurrence did actually take place, so Kat viewed this as a literal miracle that it could be found this close to home, even if it was only once a year.

Kat slid a chair over next to hers for Carrie who sat down nodding and verbalizing something that sounded like a thank you amid a full mouth.

"Mmmmm. I'm starving," she managed to say between bites. "I've been out here since 5:30 a.m. this morning, checking people into their booths and I think my head hit the pillow somewhere around 2:00 a.m. by the time we finished painting the numbers for each booth onto the street. I've been running up and down the street all day, smelling everything. I figured I was on the brink of committing a felony if I didn't get something to eat. It was time for some food!"

"I know," Kat said with a smile. "Carrie and Kat get *cwabby* when they don't eat!"

Carrie nodded her full agreement, shoveling another piping-hot bite into her mouth. She fanned and waved at her mouth looking around for something to drink. One of the kids handed her a red can of black cherry-flavored seltzer water from an obliging cooler, and without bothering to look at it, she took a long swig. A moment later, after she had recovered from the near miss "barba-charcoaling" of the entire length of her esophagus, she looked at the can, her face twisted in disgust.

"What the devil is this slop? It tastes like TV static! If TV static had a taste, this would be it—Wow! Whose bright idea was this?! It's like drinking a glass of water and someone in the next room is shouting Black Cherry at you!" Carrie finished sputtering.

She turned back to her lunch, hoping to get the formidable taste out of her mouth. Everyone else was practically choking themselves, though with laughter at Carrie's unexpected fit and version of popular Facebook content.

Carrie was the daughter of The Voice and a very busy member of the community club, instrumental in making sure that everything went off without a hitch. Her phone began ringing in May, arranging booths and other details. It didn't stop until the day after the September event. She and Nancy wore bright hot pink baseball caps with the Sheep Drive logo of years past on them so they could be easily spotted in the crowd. Each time someone needed assistance with parade entries or booths etc., they would be directed to find the ladies in the pink hats. With Nancy's six-foot-tall stature and fire-engine red hair, she was especially easy to pick out, even in the large crowd.

When all else failed, The Voice could be called upon to summon people to the places they were needed. What might sound like code to the crowd, like "Carrie, clean up aisle six," was just The Voice's clever way of directing them to where they needed to be, even if it meant a stop by the stage for specific instructions. By late afternoon, their duties would be fulfilled and then, they too, could sit and relax, marking off yet another successful Sheep Drive in the books.

The Sheep Drive logo chosen for hats and t-shirts changed each year, with some manner of humorous picture of a sheep or a play on the word Ewe, but since the pink-hat strategy had been so wildly successful for locating their two best agents, the girls kept them for each coming year. They would bring along another hat and clothes for later, and the official removal of the pink hat, meant their day was done. The hat was then hung up, retired from duty until the following year.

After eating their lunch and visiting for a little while, the Pattersons headed back down the street to load up horses for the short journey home. They would no doubt be happy to be free of their stations and enjoy a long, cool drink.

They were back just in time for the late afternoon grand finale event. The log-sawing contest kept the crowd captive for the full day, as nobody wanted to miss it. Sam, along with about every other able-bodied male in town, was a regular participant. The ladies would have their own competition, as well as the opportunity to participate as a mixed team.

There were a couple of sisters in town who routinely gave all the men a run for their money. They were tall and slender compared to some of the muscle-bound guys that stepped up to the plate, but they had been doing this all their lives, and were so flawless in their teamwork, they made it look like running a knife through soft butter. It was an event that looked like it would be won by brute strength, but it was finesse that would prove victorious.

Operation of the two-man crosscut saw required endurance and skillful pulling. Each side had to take a turn pulling the saw in their direction and then ease their grip and allow it to be pulled away from them. Any attempt to push the saw would make it bow in the center, causing the teeth to come out of the grooves being cut in the log. It would then catch and get hung up until someone pulled it out and set it back in the groove, all of which would be continually adding seconds to the team's time. As an added bonus, there could also be knots in the log at any given position that could cause the saw to hang up and require some extra time to get through.

Teams of sawyers were registering at the stage. The Voice was also now finished with her day and had turned the microphone over to another well-known personality that would auction the teams off during a spirited calcutta, as well as announce all the teams and their times. Again, cash prizes, now dependent on the amount the team was sold for, would be awarded for the fastest three times.

Kat settled into a chair on Main Street, ready to video this year's attempt at the first- place prize. Sam was standing behind her, too twitchy with excitement to sit still in a chair. His ringing cell phone cut off whatever it was he had just bent down to say.

"Hello. Yes, this is Sam Patterson. Really?! You gotta be kidding me! Ok, we're on our way."

Kat leaned back in her chair looking up at Sam behind her. He was already gone. She stood up to look around and caught sight of his bright pink shirt making his way to the stage. He spoke briefly to the auctioneer and then hurried back to her.

"We have to go; that was the county dispatch. We have cows out on the road."

Kat's heart fell, and the boys groaned, knowing the day of fun was over. It was one of the price tags hung on their lifestyle and where they lived. It wasn't written even in fine print on the contract; it was just a given, something that everyone knew.

The working day was daylight to dark, and into the middle of the night when necessary. The work week never ended. Every day was Monday. The fact that the kind of work they could not ignore could interrupt anything in their lives both day and night was always present. Kat said she was well suited for her job because she grew up this way, and it was essentially the same in the medical field. Illness and injury did not have respect for weekends, holidays, the middle of the night or the simple fact that you would like to be done at 5:00 a.m. to go home to have dinner with your family.

People often refer to nurses as the angels of mercy. While it was a pretty notion, and she surely knew some great ones, Kat always felt the cowboy was the best example of God's unsung heroes. He was given a heart that had more room for love and joy than one could imagine, as well as the ability to appreciate a simple life with basic provision and little need for frills.

He respects the land and every life put on it, with a genuine willingness to trade his own for the ones he is entrusted with. His first love was Mother Nature, giving part of his heart to her in reverence for the beauty of every season he encountered. Every sunset and starry sky he beheld, he found to be more breathtaking than the last, though his only outright show of appreciation might just be a deep breath of the clear evening air and a quiet nod of true contentment and satisfaction in a day well done.

He would spend hours in forty-below-zero weather trying to save a single calf found frozen to the ground, keeping it warm inside his own coat until someplace warmer could be found and then rub warmth and function back into its stiff body. He would stay with it through the night, painstakingly administering fluids drop by drop into its mouth until it regained the strength to stand on its own again, taking a break only to go back out into the cold to search for more that might need his help.

In truth, God could not have created any better model of a humble servant of both land and man than when He made a cowboy. In the middle of a saddle horse, under the big sky, in his mind, he was already in heaven, ever walking there with the Man Upstairs—something the rest of us haven't managed to do since Adam and Eve left the garden. There is certainly testimony that they can be a little rough around the edges, but no more than anyone else. They might twist a cork, chew tobacco and use bad language, but they will always look you square in the eye and deal you a straight hand. They will tell you the hard truth—to your face instead of the back of your head when nobody else would—and then stand there to hear what you might have to say on the subject. They will own their faults and take any cussin' they know they have coming, answering only with a sincere apology and a genuine desire to do better next time, making no excuses for what happened.

Sam's face was a combination of resignation and urgency to get going. His *It is what it is* mentality had already taken over, and he had moved on to getting the job done. There were no complaints, no sighs, no fuss; he just pressed on.

The redhead in Kat was screaming on the inside, practically pitching a fit and falling in it at the unfair and rotten timing of this development and probably concerning walkabout cattle in general. *Why on this day of all days?!* Kat fumed in her head.

She knew she had better get a handle on it if she was going to keep her outward attitude in check. She had to work extremely hard to mirror Sam's calm countenance and was thankful that he put forth such model behavior to draw from. The control freak in her hated changes in plans with a purple passion. Sam was always a "roll with the punches" kind of personality. If he had gotten upset and started complaining, it would have been nearly impossible for her to not jump right on the bandwagon with him and commiserate about it all the way home. Instead, she knew they needed to leave immediately, so she looked around making sure everyone was present and they all headed off to the pickup.

Sam's long-legged stride made his steps twice as long as everyone else's and nearly three steps for Kasi-Ann on a normal day, much less when he was in a hurry. It was yet to be seen if she would inherit her father's height, or if she swam a little too long in Kat's gene pool—which in Kat's opinion could use a lifeguard and some chlorine. She hoped Kasi-Ann would not be of shorter stature like her mother, but there was certainly no changing whatever was to be, no matter the amount of wishing or hoping.

"C'mon," she gestured to the kids with her hand and took off faster, practically running to catch up to Sam.

"We have runaway cows, Kasi-Ann! What would Camo Girl do?" she asked, trying to brighten her own mood by changing the perspective of the situation into being an adventure.

"She'd ride as fast as lightning to where they were and round them all up—turn em' back to the gate!" she answered running full steam for the pickup.

"Atta girl!" Kat cheered, now hearing more of a genuine smile in her voice.

It was uncertain how many cows were out, how far they had traveled from their temporary home since the fire, or what it would take to get them all back together behind the fence again. What they did know was that they were reported to be out on a well-traveled road, and the risk of their injury and death, or that of the unsuspecting driver who hit them was cause enough for Sam to break the speed limit getting there.

CHAPTER 11

# Keep On Truckin'

A beautiful Montana fall extravaganza was ablaze with color before anyone had time to realize that summer was gracefully bowing out. It seemed like the orange, crimson and yellow leaves on the trees along the river arrived almost overnight. Now the frost on the pumpkin was showing up on a regular basis and getting heavier each morning. The crisp smell and feel of the air promised cooler weather every day, bidding the warmer afternoons of a lingering Indian summer a fond farewell.

Kat had barely had time to notice the changes going on outside. This was the time of year that she became a single parent with a switch-hit sitter on speed dial. Mr. Bevolden was an absolute Godsend to their family during this season. September officially marked the "fall run" that sent Sam and his trusty iron horse Half Painted all over creation, hauling fat cattle. The first to go were their own, now that the fire had torched the fences.

Thankfully, there even hadn't been time to stand there and think about what that really meant long enough to have it sink in. He unloaded his life's work at the sale barn and then loaded someone else's cows, headed for Nebraska that same morning.

There wasn't any other option, so it didn't warrant discussing in Sam's mind, he just drove on, thankful that he still had provision to make a living with, and a responsibility to keep his mind occupied.

He would be gone for weeks at a time with barely time to eat, get clean clothes, and sleep in his own bed for a night before he was back on the road. Even then, almost every time he made it home, he would be up half the night with the truck in the shop, fixing things he didn't have the luxury of addressing on the road, so he could go again in the morning. He was his own mechanic and fixed most of the ailments on Half Painted himself, unless it was something that rendered it inoperable while he was away from home.

He'd learned to operate on a handful of hours of sleep per week, some of which were not voluntarily achieved. He liked to think he had trained himself to fall asleep at the drop of a hat whenever the truck was stopped, whether it was a delay in getting loaded or waiting in line to be unloaded, but in all honesty, the continual state of bone-weary exhaustion facilitated instant sleep whenever his eyes closed.

He had lots of buddies on the road driving with him that kept him company on the CB radio when he felt like his eyes were in danger of snapping shut against his will. He was drinking coffee by the gallons, operating out of three tall, green, Coleman thermoses at a time, though he was suspicious that the effect caffeine had on him was steadily deteriorating.

He was currently headed north on Highway 85, empty, after another round of the "Fort Morgan 500," hauling fat cattle to the Excel packing house in Colorado. The wind had picked up and was making a real nuisance of itself for his partner, Lee. Compared to Sam's heavier Wilson cattle trailer, his Guthrie was taking a beating, and all the wheels on the side of the trailer taking the brunt of the wind had already caught some air a couple times. Without the weight of the cattle, the empty trailer was like a sitting duck, waiting to be knocked over by the next big gust, possibly taking the truck over with it.

In an effort to give him some wind relief, Sam moved over to the hammer lane and slowed down, allowing Lee to come right up beside him, effectively blocking the wind. There hadn't been any traffic to speak of, giving them a clear shot at both sides of the road. They were chatting back and forth about the last load and the prospect of having a couple days to lie down and sleep for a month when another truck ahead of them crested a hill and apparently noticed their formation behind him.

"Evenin,' northbound bull haulers," a gravelly voice broke in over the radio. "Name's Earl. I just wanted to let you know I see what you have going on back there. I don't know about you, but I think the wind might blow!" he added with a friendly boisterous chuckle. "I've got my eyes on a wide-open road up here, and I'll be sure to let you know of anything that changes that."

"10–4, pard,' very much appreciated," Sam answered back. She's a little push come to shove back here, for sure."

"Sure wish I had a cup of coffee," Lee mentioned settling back in his chair, relaxing a bit more knowing there were eyes out in front of them.

"I'm only on thermos number two if ya need a fill up," Sam offered.

"Well sure!" Lee said, rolling down his window. "Let er' rip tater chip."

Sam rolled down his passenger side window, steadied his left hand on the wheel and gave the thermos and toss with his right.

It made a perfect landing right into Lee's outstretched hands. He filled his oversized travel mug driving one handed and then took a second to aim for the thermos's return flight. He made another right on target toss, landing the thermos squarely in Sam's passenger seat.

Earl's deep belly laugh broke through on the radio a second time. "You two didn't just do what I think you just did ... did ya?" he asked, continuing to laugh. "I looked in the mirror and saw something go flying from one truck to the other, and then a couple minutes later it came back. Did you *really* just throw your thermos back and forth?!"

"Yup. When a feller needs coffee, he needs coffee," Sam replied. "Let the record show, I'm not one to stand in between a man and his coffee ... or drive in between it for that matter," Sam said, now chuckling himself. "Hey Lee, let's not tell Kat about this one though, huh?"

High-pitched hysterical laughter was all that was audible from Lee before he at last came back with a half choked, "10–4."

They drove on chatting and listening for warnings from Earl that never surfaced. It was smooth sailing all the way. Earl bowed out at Cheyenne, wishing them well as they continued north every mile, making them more and more antsy to be home. It had been three weeks, five days and nineteen years since Sam had been home last. Wyoming was offering little to distract him from the miles yet to be covered.

He was mounting a considerable argument that the second coming of the Savior was sure to arrive before the sign reading Casper, Wyoming, came into view, pondering that he felt like he was a living, breathing definition of eternity. He had a list as long as his left arm of things that Half Painted needed to have fixed, adjusted, or replaced, but they were all going to have to wait. Tonight, he was going to spend time with his family.

He was able to speak to Kat and the kids on the phone from time to time, but they were busy with their schedules at home too and much of the time he wasn't available to talk when they were, or vice versa. When he found that he had time on his hands, able to talk because he was driving, not loading or loading, it was 3:00 a.m. He doubted very much Kat would see the same delusional humor he did at waking her up to tell her about the silly something or other that was currently giving him uproarious laughter because he was too tired to manage proper responses to stimuli.

Some of the jokes being told over the radio during the night were a bit off color, but still admittedly funny, though he would definitely not choose to share those with her either. It was during the late hours when it was just him and the road that he found he was bombarded with thoughts of home. He thought of her there sleeping, wondering what her day had been like.

Shaking his head, he wondered if Mr. Bevolden had been committed yet, no thanks to his youngest child's antics. If he ever thought he had his hands full with Kat's spitfire spirit, he was sadly mistaken. By the time Kasi-Ann was two, Kat's father looked her right in the eyes one day, and calmly said, "You deserve this child …" and just walked away grinning.

To coin one of Kat's favorite phrases, that little girl was a test he hadn't studied for, and he knew it would always feel like that. In kindergarten, her kindergarten teacher told them that she was "wise beyond her own well-being." It had been said slowly and matter-of-factly, so as not to confuse it with something complimentary. He had expected her report card to say "runs with scissors" or some other manner of the usual unruly behavioral stunts, but he did not quite know what to make of this description. The first-year teacher did not elaborate, but Kat later pointed out that she suspected the two had been engaged in a mind game of sorts, and Kasi-Ann had clearly bested her, much to her disliking. A hasty review of the chain of command at school, along with Kasi-Ann's position within the system was thoroughly outlined, including the fact that she did not always have to be right—even if she was.

She was definitely going to keep him on his toes, but he wouldn't trade her for the world. She had a heart of gold and a fire deep down inside of her that the world would never quench. It was the kind that people were born with, not something that could be instilled in someone, no matter how much desire and effort was applied.

His mind wandered back and forth over his sons, considering their similarities, and yet how they were truly unique and different. He appreciated how they each did their best to fill his shoes when he was away, taking responsibility for the work that had to be done whether their father was home or not. This load was considerably lightened of late with the cattle being sold, but he doubted it was any less of a load on their hearts than it was on his when the stray thoughts of the immense changes the fire had brought found them idle.

He loved their fierce sense of loyalty to one another and how they always had each other's back. He wondered if things were going well with their schoolwork. He was proud of how well rounded and respectful his boys were of everyone, especially their mother. He had no concerns whatsoever that if things were not up to par, Kat would become The Warden if necessary. She was the only woman he had ever known that could make him cringe from a verbal accosting, and for that matter, it didn't even have to be his own. He had a genuinely equal empathy for anyone else found to be on the receiving end of it, despite the fact that she would never read the riot act to anyone who hadn't truly earned it. But the fact remained that the hounds of hell looked like lap dogs compared to Kat with a real mad on, and he wouldn't wish it on his greatest enemy, man or beast.

He settled on knowing they would work hard to keep up their grades because neither one of them would risk missing out on playing football, He then frowned wondering how many games he had missed already. That thought was practically tackled and shoved aside by the immediate need to find out what day it was. He realized if asked, he couldn't be 100 percent positive that he could report the correct month, much less the current date. His tired eyes were straining to read the little date square on the wristwatch he always wore palm side down.

It was Friday. Friday! He couldn't remember if they discussed where the games were this weekend when he had spoken to Kat earlier, but he did know there was at least one home game. With a second glance at his watch, he was doing the mental math of how many hours it would take to get home, this time with several more neurons firing from the added excitement. Another realization hit him like a bolt of lightning, and he reached up to grab the coiled CB mic from its hanger.

"Lee, where do the boys play tonight?" he asked, remembering that his youngest son was in Brett's class and also on the football team.

"They're playing at 6:30 p.m. in Reed, why?" Lee asked.

"'Cause we need to get there, that's why!" Sam answered back, mashing on the throttle. "Stick your foot in it, man; we didn't come to play Barbies."

Sam knew Kat wouldn't have told the boys that he was coming home, or at least not by any certain time, because the nature of the job had too many variables that he had absolutely no control over. A couple-hour local cattle-hauling job, for example, took the better part of the day when he pulled up to where he was supposed to load from and found a saddle horse in the corral, indicating he was also going to have to gather them as well. It was a rare occurrence of course, and the rancher knew Sam very well. He would never have tolerated such circumstances from anyone other than a friend, but it was one of many scenarios where the job did not go as expected. In fact, he had stopped expecting anything to turn out a certain way years ago. It had probably saved him a lifetime of frustration.

The wind had finally calmed down and they were easily traveling along, making good time on the interstate.

*****

Kat was up to her eyebrows in patients. It was another typical Friday afternoon when people came out of the woodwork, faced with the prospect of having to now wait until Monday to be seen for something that had been ailing them since last Christmas. Two of the three secretaries did their best to only add on patients with genuinely emergent needs, but the one doing the bulk of the scheduling, who of course always left on time, acted like she got a personal bonus for every patient seen and didn't care in the slightest if she booked the nurses an hour past the end of their shifts for a simple blood pressure check.

The clinic staffed one doctor and one nurse practitioner, closing at 5:00 p.m. most days of the week, with one late clinic on

Monday that ended at 7:00 p.m. Kat and the other nurse Daisy now rotated, working for both the doctor and the nurse, as well as trading who had to work the late clinic every other week.

Daisy Devereaux was a beautiful African American, southern bell from Alabama who had come to town as a traveling nurse to fill the position vacated by a lady who had been there since the day the clinic was built and opened its doors. From the pictures that hung on the wall of the original staff and building, she had been 100 years old then. Sam had known her his whole life and liked to tease that when she was a kid the Dead Sea was still sick. When she retired, even she admitted she couldn't remember how many years she had been there, so when asked, she'd simply say, "*All* of them." Kat had gleaned much from her in the twelve years they worked together.

Daisy had only intended to stay a few months until a more permanent candidate could be found, but she tripped and fell in love with a local business owner, literally. She had gone into his establishment to have lunch one day, and when it was time to leave, she tripped on an upturned corner of the rug at the door, twisting her ankle. The owner saw it happen and rushed out to help her. He picked her up and returned her to the clinic, this time as a patient herself. He later confessed that he had wanted to come out and meet her but felt a little shy about just brazenly coming over to her table.

The shyness was a temporary affliction once he realized she was hurt. Within a couple of months of the incident, Daisy asked about taking the position and staying on permanently. It had been three years since then. Kat adored working with her and was positively tickled pink that she decided to stay. They worked so well together they finished each other's thoughts and sentences, sometimes before they were started. Kat would poke her head out of an exam room to ask for something, only to have Daisy standing there with what she needed already in her hand. It was delightful to have another young, high-energy nurse in the ranks.

They were standing in the hall with all the patient rooms full, waiting for the physician and practitioner to wade through them, just so they could load up another wave. Kat was sharing her excitement that Sam was hopefully headed home for a few days plus all of their other weekend plans, between Halloween and football games.

Daisy was listening and looking over the newest printed version of their "already been changed a hundred times" schedule for the afternoon, frowning at the newly added appointments. It was the nature of the beast for a rural clinic, serving multiple surrounding communities. Many of the patients did not present emergency room-level needs, but there was often a lack of planning on the general public's part that became the clinic's emergency when they wanted prescriptions renewed at 4:30 p.m. on Friday. Or at least this was Joe Public's view of the situation anyway.

The closest trauma center-level ER was about fifty miles away and there were occasionally things that came through the door that were just bandaged up or stabilized enough to make the rest of that journey.

"Seriously!? An allergy shot at 4:55 p.m.? I swear to heaven that woman is pure evil, Kat," Daisy exclaimed, still glaring at the schedule like she was daring it to change again. "An' if I hear her say *bless their little cotton socks* one more time, I'm gonna beat her with her own broom… Woman wouldn't know a blessing if it slapped her up the backside o' her own fool head," Daisy continued with a look of disdain. "Well, I'll stay the extra half hour to make sure the allergy shot doesn't have any reactions; you gotta get home to Sam!"

Wanda Wynn-Wilson would not exactly be described as a glass half full individual. She had a face best suited for radio and a disposition to match. A hoarse whiskey baritone voice from decades of smoking and a tongue that dripped pure, high-octane negativity were just a couple of the accessory services she provided. She delighted in bringing up every mistake anyone ever made, or telling unfavorable stories about people, usually because she believed it somehow personally wronged her and she ended the story with "bless their little cotton socks." It was spit out like a blasphemy, not as an excuse for their behavior, on their behalf, or hers for that matter. If the story was particularly juicy, or she was even more perturbed than usual by something someone had done, it would conjure a "bless their little *white* cotton socks," with considerable emphasis on the white. Sadly, if the woman were a song, her name would be "I Love to Tell the Story," and it was far from The Good News.

The middle-aged pot stirrer was never happy to begin with and never happiest than when dragging someone through the mud. She would argue for the simple sake of argument and fed on strife like a blood-thirsty vampire, though the villain she was most often referred to around the office matched her own initials: The Wicked Witch of the West.

This afternoon was no exception. She had already come swooping through the nurse's station a couple of times, spreading hate and discontent like trick or treat candy, sparing no one. At one point, Daisy took off following her with what looked like genuine intent to wring her neck, until Kat grabbed her by the back of her scrub shirt. She actually struggled against her for a second and then came to her senses, settling on shrieking, "And your little dog too!" about the time Wanda was out of earshot.

"C'mon, Kat, I was only gonna kill her a little bit. I'd be doing us all a favor ... kill her dead and say she just died. Honest, she was dead when I got here..." she went on.

"You don't mean that," Kat said, not even attempting to keep the smile off her face. Daisy's tangled version of honesty and humor always cracked her up.

"Besides, you have to drop a house on her or drown her in a bucket of water, remember?" Kat chided.

"I jus' don't understand why she gotta be like that, all up in our faces raining down flying monkeys an' stuff," Daisy said, looking a little deflated.

"Some people just don't know how to be happy, Daisy. They don't even realize that they are making themselves the most miserable, and misery loves company, so somehow, they want everyone else to be miserable too. Can you imagine her poor husband? He has to put up with that every day of his life! He's been locked in a room with the never-ending hourglass since he said 'I do,' poor devil!"

"Now that's the Hallelujah Truth right there, sugar!" Daisy exclaimed pointing at her in agreement.

"Well, however she does go, those ruby red slippers are *mine!* Probably don't look good on her anyway," Daisy said walking down to the last patient room where the nurse practitioner had just stepped out.

She turned halfway down the hall and gave Kat a big wink. Her smile and sense of humor now indicated she had possibly moved past any witch-hunt tendencies and was once again focused on getting through their patients.

Just then, Dr. James opened the door from exam room 2 and presented Kat with a long list of x-rays and lab tests for the patient who sounded as though they were doing their best to cough up a lung behind him.

There was no more time to banter back and forth about their resident broom-bearing co-worker, there was work to do, and literally a foot race to the end of the day to get it all done in time to leave. She was thankful that Daisy had already volunteered to stay late so she could leave at 5:00 p.m., no matter what else came through the door or took longer than expected between then and now. She could hardly contain her excitement about Sam being home tonight, whistling a cheery tune as she escorted her still-coughing patient down to the lab. She was beginning to sound more like a barking seal, making Kat's own chest ache in sympathy.

She went back down the hall and began setting up a nebulizer breathing treatment, just as the doctor came out of another room saying, "We should also give Mrs. Jackson a breathing ... never mind, I see you're already on it. Thanks, Kat," he finished and quickly disappeared again behind the door of exam room 4.

It was 5:30 p.m. when Kat finally walked out to her vehicle to leave with Daisy all but physically shoving her out the door. She wished her a Happy Halloween and locked the clinic back door behind her. Even if Kat had forgotten something, she would have to live without it until Monday. She knew the dangers of coming back for something and ending up being there another hour. Kat was hard enough to get out the door, she wasn't taking any chances.

Fighting the guilt of leaving Daisy there with patients, Kat forced herself to drive out of the parking lot and point the pickup toward home. She knew every inch of the twenty-five-mile drive like the back of her hand, but she made a great effort to try to pick out something new in the scenery, as well as to visually recognize certain points along the way. The alternative was to arrive home after some level of a hypnotic trance, realizing that she didn't remember driving most of the way home. It was always both chilling and somewhat remorseful that she could go through the motions of driving home and still have no marked memory of it.

What beauty of the season or time of day had she missed? What had she failed to witness that might have made a lasting impression or memory? It was something her mother had taught her about life being more of a journey than a destination. There was something for us to find at every step, not just at the point where we wished to go.

Those thoughts faded as she turned down the long drive and one by one, the three four-legged welcoming committee fell into step, chasing the pickup. Two were confirmed tire biters, with the lack of a couple bottom teeth to prove it, while the other was still on the fence, constantly charging them, backing off at the last minute, with a mixed expression of terror and "Just kidding …"

This one was his own special breed of idiot. More often than not, in his infinite wisdom, he felt it was better to run along in *front* of the vehicle, so close that you couldn't see him over the hood, as opposed to alongside. The last portion of the driveway, being considerably more uphill, often required a little more effort on the vehicle's part to make the top. When the snow started to stick, Sam would be seen making two if not three attempts at the ascent because Kenworth would insist on running along in front.

When Sam could not see him or had any concern that he wasn't running fast enough, he would slow down, thereby getting stuck in the driveway. He would then have to back down to the flat portion and make another attempt. By the second go, Sam would have lost his patience over the ordeal, and it was every man for himself, never mind that this was a blatant infraction of the "stay back" rule on the dog's part. Kenworth understood the memo to get back when the horses all had legs and riders, but the fool critter was forever trying to outrun the several hundred that lived under the hood.

If Sam actually had to make a third run at it, he was planning to "just give er' the onion," and make the top of the hill come hell or high tide. Even the wackadoodle dog got the memo to stand back when he revved the engine like an Indy racer and dumped the clutch. With a snow-flurrying finish, he was lucky to come to a stop without driving through the garage wall on the other side.

Kat saw Mr. Bevolden standing on the porch, waving a greeting as she pulled in. It was going to be a rush to get changed and get Kasi-Ann gathered up so they could make it back to town for the football game.

"How goes the battle today?" Mr. Bevolden inquired, holding the door for her while she carried her things into the house.

She had to skirt around the newly relocated jack-o-lanterns on the top step to get in the door. They were lounging on the back porch this morning when she had left, but she figured Kasi-Ann had done some redecorating.

"Helter skelter ... You'd think it was Friday the 13th instead of just Halloween, but I suppose I should be grateful it's not both right?" Kat asked, sounding as weary as she looked.

"True that, madam, true that," he said with mild conviction. "Kasi-Ann has had her dinner. She has her costume in a bag here by the door along with her snowsuit. She doesn't believe a word my old bones say, in fact we had a sizable dispute about whether or not they even speak English, but I have a left shoulder that is practically shouting about a snowstorm that is doing its best to sneak up on us at any minute. Been mumbling about it for the last three days, until this afternoon when it became quite convinced and hasn't shut up about it since," he qualified rubbing the offending shoulder with his hand.

"What did she decide on for a costume?" Kat asked over her shoulder, as she was putting the contents of an untouched lunch back into the refrigerator.

She walked from there down the short hallway to her bedroom to change clothes. Mr. Bevolden knew the drill. He waited in the kitchen while she tossed her uniforms into the hamper, opened and shut drawers, finding jeans and a school team sweatshirt to put on before rejoining him. Then she went to the sink and washed thoroughly all the way up to her elbows, grabbing a paper towel by the corner with a wet finger and thumb to wipe them dry with. It was the same procedure every time. The minute she got home, her scrubs came off and went into the dirty clothes bin that only her work clothes touched. She would not hug or hold any of the children until she had removed them and washed whatever might be left of her workday off. It was nearly as automatic as breathing.

"She changed her mind, and her clothes, no less than seventy-five times, I believe, finally settling on being a witch. I also parked the broom of her choice next to her bag, but I told her it would be up to you whether or not it got to tag along," he finished with a gentle smile.

Kat noticed he looked a bit weary as well. "If your shoulder is truly giving you trouble, I could get you into the doctor for a cortisone shot. It can take a week or so to really kick in, but they can do wonders," Kat offered, with mounting concern.

"Oh, don't you be worrying about me when you have a ball game to be getting yourselves to," he replied. "Now, scoot!" he said, gesturing toward the door, closing the discussion on the subject.

Kat frowned at him for dismissing her, but knew he was right about them needing to leave. She hollered for Kasi-Ann to get her things so they could go. She came bounding down the stairs two at a time. It made Kat's stomach twist into knots, thinking about the crash that would ensue if she tripped, but she elected to write the worry off with a reminder that children are practically made of rubber for the better part of their formative years for this very purpose.

"Hi, Mom!" Kasi-Ann shouted and kept right on going, grabbing her costume bag and broom in one fluid motion.

She ran out the door to the car, her gracefulness apparently ceasing there, as she tried to get into the car with the broom nearly sideways. Two attempts at repositioning the broom finally permitted entry, and she was seated and buckled, less than patiently awaiting her mother. Mr. Bevolden was looking a bit sympathetically at her now, silently comparing keeping Kasi-Ann in line to the prospect of herding cats, suddenly feeling as tired as he looked.

"Well, if you change your mind, let me know. Have a good evening, and thank you for all your help," Kat said as she gave Mr. Bevolden a gentle hug, trying to be mindful of his shoulder.

"Of course," he replied. "As always, it is my pleasure. Enjoy yourselves and tell the boys I said good luck. I will see you Sunday morning."

"I will. See you Sunday," Kat said, closing the door behind her.

Getting in the car, she couldn't quite get her mind off his shoulder complaint for some reason. Perhaps it was more so that her perception of his "ache" seemed to run deeper than an arthritic shoulder. She couldn't help but wonder if he was lonely; she knew she would be in his shoes. His wife had been gone since Kasi-Ann was a baby, after all. She knew better than to try to play Cupid, but she would have to confess that she did do a quick mental run of all the single ladies in their parish and surrounding area. Knowing she needed to concentrate on the drive into town, she conceded to tabling the issue until at least Sunday when she could do a visual headcount of the potential prospects. A bit of a devilish smile began to sneak across her face, as she put her focus back on the road.

They arrived at the school, quickly parked and dashed out to the football field. The crisp, October evening air was full of excitement as the teams lined up along the field in preparation for the national anthem. Just as Kat was beginning to wonder of Sam's whereabouts, the cell phone in her back pocket began ringing. With the distraction of Mr. Bevolden and the drive, she had completely forgotten to check in on his progress.

"Hi, honey!" Kat said.

"Hi, baby, how are ya?"

"I'm great, how 'bout you?" she answered and asked back.

"Oh, not so bad, I guess."

It was his usual reply. His truck could be on fire with him in it but his laid-back nature would answer back, *Oh, not so bad, I guess...*

"Where are you? The game is just about to start."

"Oh good, I'm just coming over the hill. I'll let them know I'm here, and I'll see you in a bit," he said excitedly and hung up without saying goodbye.

She had no idea what that meant, until two minutes later when, just as the anthem finished, Half Painted, Lee, and five other cow trucks came down the hill right in front of the field and laid on the air horns. Sam had installed a train horn on Half Painted, and the boys instantly recognized the sound.

Their heads flew around toward the interstate where the convoy of drivers Sam had talked to and asked to line up and honk to salute the team came into view seconds later. Their faces lit up and the hometown crowd erupted in cheering, seeing Sam and Lee returning home. They came down the exit and pulled the trucks into the sawmill lot next door to the school, arriving on the field minutes later.

Kasi-Ann came running from playing with her friends on the grassy hill beyond the end zone at the sound of Half Painted's signature horn. Each time Sam rolled into the drive after being gone, he would sound the loud horn signifying his return.

"Daddy!" She hollered as she caught sight of him coming in the gates. She ran and jumped in his arms, giving him a big hug.

He scooped her up and kept right on walking, his eyes fixed on the little redhead coming toward him from midfield. He wrapped his free arm around her waist and hauled her up against him, giving her a quick kiss on the cheek. Then he put her down a second later and scanned the field. The boys were waiting for him. Their eyes met and Sam gave them an "I'm here" nod. It was all they needed. They nodded in return and turned back into the huddle.

"Okay, ladies, hang up your purses; it's time to go to work," Bret said as the team stepped into formation for the kickoff.

Kat closed her eyes for a moment, thinking it felt more like Christmas than Halloween. Sam was home and she had the whole weekend to enjoy her family. Almost as though he could hear her thinking, which he somehow often did, he gave her a little squeeze with the arm that was still around her and no apparent intentions of letting her go anytime soon. That was just perfect in her mind.

Even Kasi-Ann stood on the other side clutching her father's hand, content to hold onto him and his undivided attention instead of returning immediately to her playmates. She was simultaneously using his left arm as her own personal jungle gym and talking up a storm. It was another 100 mile-per-hour recount of everything that had happened since Sam had been gone, from her Halloween costume, the renegade rooster, some of the dogs' shenanigans and one or two of the boys' infractions. Sam realized a long time ago he couldn't listen as fast as she could talk, so he did his best to summarize most of it in his mind and figured on working out the details later.

At half time, the home team had a sizable lead, and given that it was Halloween, there was still the trick or treating that Kasi-Ann was looking forward to, yet to take place. There was no way she was going to miss it, so Kat helped get her costume out of the car and put it on. She was so excited that her dad got to see it. They stood in the school parking lot, getting Kasi-Ann and her costume situated, looking around at all the other vehicles. Kat was fairly certain that nearly everyone in town was at the game, so the prospects of going door to door might be quite limited, but it would not a bad thing if she didn't end up with a bushel barrel of junk food either. Some of the town's residents were famous for handing out full-sized chocolate bars.

Sam told Kasi-Ann he would like to watch more of the game, but he would at least go with them and walk around a couple blocks with her, so they took off walking down the next block from the school, stopping at the houses on the south side of the street. Kasi-Ann had her broom and her orange plastic pumpkin bucket for collecting goodies in her left hand, with her father's oversized hand wrapped around the right. She was the happiest witch on the scene.

As expected, there were not many people home, but each door or porch had a bowl of candy left for the taking in their absence. Kasi-Ann walked up to each one, still saying trick or treat, choosing one item from the offerings, saying thank you, and walking back out to the street to join her parents, regardless of whether or not anyone was there. She even offered to share her goodies with her brothers when she got home since they didn't get to go with her this year. Kat thanked her and told her it was very kind to be so generous and then stuck her free hand in her pocket, fighting back the urge to clap it over the child's forehead under that pointed witch's hat and assess her for fever.

The cheers from the football field could be heard echoing down the block. Halftime had concluded, and they were well into the third quarter when they arrived back at the school. Kasi-Ann's apparent fever-induced madness even went as far as squelching her desire to continue beyond the ten houses they had visited, so she and her half full pumpkin were willing to retire for the evening as well. She really didn't even rummage through everything that was in there, though with many of the self-serve stations, Kat figured that was due to the fact that she already knew what she had chosen.

Usually when you arrive, they just drop something into your bucket then half the surprise is waiting to get home and see what you ended up with. It was also wonderfully comforting to know all the people in town. You didn't have to worry about what was being handed out to children. They were all trustworthy and kind, and the only ill effects their treats would have on anyone is a bellyache or cavity—both clearly the recipient's fault for overindulging or neglecting proper dental hygiene.

The game was over half an hour later with the help of a continuously running clock. It was the effect of the mercy rule after an opponent was fifty or more points ahead. Mr. Bevolden's snowstorm had shown up at the beginning of the fourth quarter as well, so the rule proved merciful in more ways than one.

It had looked like it might end up a complete shut out, but the other team did end up with some points on the board for a Hail Mary field goal kicked on a fourth down. Their crowd acted as though they had just won the state title, and in truth, the hometown folks were so thrilled that they had finally squashed the goose egg on their side of the scoreboard, that they too cheered loudly for them. Both teams left the snowy field after shaking hands with smiles on their faces.

The Sunday morning alarm ringing in Kat's ear was about as welcome as a fox in a hen house. She could scarcely believe the weekend was winding down and tomorrow was another Monday—and her turn to do the late clinic to boot. They had played hard over the last twenty-four hours, her body was telling her it knew exactly how hard. They had traveled out of town for another football game and then played board games with the kids after they got home. It was after midnight when Kasi-Ann began to melt down, so they finished the evening by drawing names for Christmas and called it quits after that. It was their tradition to make homemade gifts each year. The idea of drawing names at Halloween was to have sufficient time to both think of and construct the gift by then.

Sam and Kat crawled into bed, listening to the boys recounting their games and hoping that the roughhousing they were hearing was a reenactment of some of the spectacular tackles Brett had.

He was already a head taller than most of the other boys with shoulders about twice as wide. With the pads and collar on he was even more intimidating, playing the position of center. If he didn't look like he meant business, one tackle was enough to make anybody an instant believer. Axel's lean agility and ability to focus under pressure were contributing toward the makings of an excellent quarterback.

Sam and Kat had talked for at least another hour after the noise upstairs had stopped. It was the first time since he had been home that they were able to enjoy a little peace and quiet, though, in truth, they had really given up on that long ago. It was probably right about the time that Kasi-Ann was born if they were being honest.

"I know I should be getting my lazy carcass out of bed and building some coffee, but this mattress is a dream come true compared to the one in the sleeper of the truck," Sam finally said.

Kat was feeling the same laziness—or was it heaviness? It felt like each of her legs weighed fifty pounds and the idea of having to swing them off the high rise, log bed and stick the landing at the bottom made her mentally assess the whereabouts of her cell phone in case a 911 call needed to be placed. She kept thinking she should already be in the shower and starting breakfast before rousting out the rest of the troops for church.

"Are you alive?" Sam asked tapping on her shoulder like a microphone to determine whether it was on or not.

"No," she groaned. "I was just thinking I should have gotten up ten minutes ago, but I think I fell asleep again before the thought process finished," she replied, snuggling back closer to his chest and under the comforter.

His arm instinctively wrapped around her and hugged her tightly, his chin coming to a rest on her left shoulder. She flinched slightly.

"Samuel, your whiskers are using my shoulder as a pin cushion. Do you suppose you might feel inclined to entertain the notion of one more round with the razor, or am I beginning my annual winter affair with Grizzly Adams again?" Kat teased.

He could practically grow facial hair on demand and elected to grow a beard each winter to protect his face against the harsh Montana cold. It wasn't gray yet, but it was obscenely bushy. His thick mustache blossomed into something that could be mistaken for a long-haired cat curled around his chin and cheeks if Kat didn't stay on him to keep it groomed regularly. She detested beards, but respected that it kept her husband warm, regarding it as *almost* a necessary evil. If she didn't trim and shape it once a week, he looked like he'd been accosted by a wild animal.

Every year he threatened to leave it alone and let it grow, just to see what it would do, but Kat finally figured out he was just saying that to ruffle her feathers, and she truly wasn't in danger of being married to Father Time. He always allowed her to trim it back when it got unruly. After a certain amount of growth, the hair changed from being a pokey, wiry texture to being soft and curly. For someone who hated beards, Kat was somehow found absentmindedly running her fingers through it and playing with the curls on more than one occasion, neither of which she was ever allowed to forget. It was fruitless to argue her opinion with Sam, as he had her caught dead to rights on the issue, but she still held her position that her preference was a state of *beardlessness*.

Sam liked to experiment with his facial hair, but Kat's favorite was his usual, namesake, Sam Elliott–style handlebar mustache.

Once he elected to shave even that off, much to the entire family's dismay. The boys were much younger, and after taking one look at him, they wrinkled their faces up and demanded that he put it back. Axel was genuinely distraught that his father looked so different. Kat informed him, in no uncertain terms, that he should never, *ever*, do that again. He had been blessed with entirely too much upper lip to let it parade around naked like that. It was borderline indecent.

"It's no-shave November," Sam said, feigning disappointment that she didn't remember.

"Oh glory," Kat mumbled back from under the heavy comforter.

She wanted to stay in bed for a month, but she knew that wasn't going to fly, so it was time to put her feet on the floor and get on with it. She was just thinking that the hot shower was doing little to fuel her decision to hit the ground running when Sam snuck in with an ice-cold glass of water and dumped it right on top of her head. She squealed like a girl, but oddly enough, suddenly she was wide awake and ready to rumble.

He left the bathroom laughing and promising her a cup of coffee when she was done. She stood there under the hot water trying to get rid of the two layers of goose bumps the ice water had provoked, promising to try not to send Captain Hilarious to heaven. She settled for plotting a suitable revenge and already knew exactly how she was going to do it. The mischievous grin that was taking over her face would simply have to ask forgiveness along with the rest of her for the devious plotting when they arrived at church in the next hour.

The service ran long as usual. It was almost noon before they returned home again. Kat had tried to whisper to Sam about Mr. Bevolden's issues, but there was no whispering that Sam was capable of hearing, especially in the left ear, after so many years of straight-piped trucks blaring at him. She gave up trying after the second time he shook his head at her, indicating he hadn't the foggiest idea what she was saying. She reached over to his bulletin and wrote *later* on it, meaning she would explain it later, in the privacy of their home, when she could talk loud enough for him and the next county to hear her.

At that point she remembered that she was going to take a mental note of the single ladies in the congregation. She visually browsed the room, coming to a stop at the third pew where the widow Mrs. Payne sat. Kat couldn't help but zero in on her hat. The poor thing had seen better days. The little bird that was supposed to be perched somewhere on top of it had slid off down to one side a bit and the feather plumes extending out of it were oddly bent and somewhat mangled in places, for lack of a better description. She wondered for a moment if her cat might have had a go at it.

Mrs. Payne, however, did not appear to be one bit concerned with it. She was giving the pastor her full attention, smiling, and nodding her agreement one moment then vehemently shaking her head no and scowling. Her expressions changed with the course of the message, though it did look as if she were having a hard time making up her mind what she really felt.

Kat always thought she looked a bit like Mrs. Peabody in the game Clue she had played as a child—a mix of nervous cluelessness and fearful suspicion. No, that would never do for Mr. Bevolden. He was sharp, very witty and enjoyed spirited conversation. It was just as likely as not he'd scare the dickens out of her by even asking if she wanted to have coffee. Even if he didn't inadvertently scare the breath out of her, there would still be the matter of whether or not she could even make up her mind to go.

She was fidgeting in her seat, looking around, as her gaze moved over the attendees a second time, it was Sam who wrote on the bulletin next, writing *focus* underneath her *later* and shoving it in front of her. She nodded in apologetic agreement turning her attention back to the pastor and the message for the day. She hadn't even read the bulletin yet to see what the title of the message was. Underneath, there was always an outline with blanks to be filled in as you followed along with the PowerPoint presentation on the overhead at the front of the church. It was helpful for later reflection during the week to look over the notes if desired. She read the headline in bold black letters on the bright orange, Halloween-themed bulletin: "Priorities: What are You Giving Your Attention To?"

She winced as though she had been poked. *Ok, God, I get it … sorry,* she thought to herself, straightening her posture and focusing in earnest this time. The pastor was her husband's cousin, which made her feel all the more guilty about her inattentive behavior.

*"Wouldn't you know, you finally get to the point where your children are all quiet and well conducted during the service, and your wife has to be told to behave,"* she could almost hear Sam telling her on the way home. Then just for a moment, before she finally began to listen intently again, her thoughts derailed one last time to her little plot for revenge on the shower attack. For good measure, she quickly prayed a silent prayer: *Forgive me, Lord. I know EXACTLY what I do.*

Sam was out in the shop ten minutes after arriving home and changing clothes. There were about ten million things on his to-do list for Half Painted, but he was going to have to settle for about six of the most important because as of 5:30 a.m. tomorrow morning, he was going to be back out on the road. Kat went to work cooking for the week so she could pack lunches and have some things to work with that allowed for putting together quick meals in the evening. Monday night Mr. Bevolden and Kasi-Ann would cook supper while he was there, looking after her until Kat got home from her late clinic. One less night to worry about cooking and cleaning up was such a blessing, not to mention that she adored his company and lively sense of humor.

They were all cut from the same cloth of overachiever cooks too, so those leftovers would make another meal later in the week as well. Even when his wife was alive, they did much of their cooking together, so Mr. Bevolden was a very knowledgeable teacher to Kasi-Ann. He came up with the idea of making dinner, not only because of the late hour that Kat got home but it was one less thing for her to do and because he celebrated Kasi-Ann's love of cooking. He was thrilled at the prospect of being able to give her a cooking lesson or at least share the joy of preparing a meal with someone—something he had genuinely mourned the loss of as much as his wife.

He did convey to Kat that she was inherently far more opinionated than his wife had been and often questioned his use of spices and so forth. He said they would sometimes have to call a truce and elect to try her method one time and his the next time then compare notes. He would also confess, somewhat begrudgingly, that her ideas had been spot-on multiple times and that perhaps he had as much to learn from her as she did from him, but he would appreciate it if she kept that information to herself.

Kasi-Ann was by far more interested in being a pastry chef, likely due to her love of dessert, but she enjoyed any time she spent in the kitchen, especially with her mother. She was less excited over learning to make gravy than pie crust, but she was an attentive learner. Mr. Bevolden figured out if he asked for her opinion about what they should make for supper, she was decidedly more interested in learning about all that he had to share about the meal. She would even make sure she went to the freezer and got out whatever meat was required for their menu before she got on the bus so it was ready for them to cook when she got home. She made a shopping list whenever necessary and would put it on the chore board so Kat could see what items needed to be purchased and be sure to pick them up.

Then because it was her specialty, she always got to choose the dessert. Whether by luck or happenstance, she expertly paired light fruity desserts with heavier meals like pastas in cream sauce and selected a richer dessert when they planned for broth-based soups and salads as the main fare.

The next adventure he had planned for her was teaching her to set a formal table with all the extra forks and falderal, as he had put it. This, however, could not take place until he had researched and brushed up on the topic himself. It was hard to imagine needing such knowledge or skills in the little corner of the world that they called home in Montana, but he knew Kasi-Ann would be limitless. It would not surprise him one bit to see her leave town and take the culinary world by storm. She was the very essence of the all-or-nothing kind of committed, and he couldn't wait to see what she did with the passion already driving such a young, fearless heart.

Kat was pulling hot apple pie turnovers and lasagna out of the oven when Sam came back to the house, inquisitively mumbling about where the hours of a single day seem to go.

"Something smells delicious," Sam said as his eyes discovered the trays of turnovers cooling on top of the stove.

He reached out to sample a piece and found his hand firmly slapped by Kat who was, just a second ago over a foot away, engaged in chopping greens for a salad to accompany dinner. She hadn't even looked up, and then went right on chopping another second later.

"Ow, jeez, how do you do that? You didn't even stop chopping …" he asked, bewildered, shaking a hand that really didn't hurt.

"Go wash your paws," Kat said with sympathetic amusement in her voice. "Where are the boys?"

"They're right behind me, I think," Sam replied, still looking at her like she had just performed some magical feat, and he was afraid to look away for fear of missing the next one or having it hit him squarely in the head this time. "They just finished giving the truck a good scrubbing inside and out."

As promised, the porch door opened, and two soaking-wet river rats stepped into the mud room. They looked at their father and then immediately looked down at their feet.

"His fault," Axel mumbled as he hurriedly began peeling off his wet boots and jacket.

"What?! No!" Brett interjected, and gave Axel a small shove.

Axel promptly shoved him back, both of them breaking out in laughter and grunting as they hit the floor in a dripping tangle, wrestling around. Brett's head got smashed up against an old pair of Sam's boots as he was jockeying for a better hold on Axel's free arm. The hand on the end of that free arm was doing an adequate job of poking him in the ribs as his lanky long legs were wrapped around Brett's waist. He was sufficiently pinned between the bench and his brother, but he had the benefit of brute strength enough to hold Axel right where he wanted him until he'd had a moment to consider his options. He outweighed his little brother by an easy twenty pounds, but what he lacked in stature, Axel made up for in tenacity. He was by no means giving an inch, but he too rested a moment while Brett was thinking.

Meanwhile, without saying a word, Sam had opened the mudroom door wide so that he and Kat now had a front row seat at the spontaneous WWF match that was taking place. This was almost an everyday occurrence, so Sam could already guess at what happened with the pressure washer and five-gallon bucket of soapy water being used to wash Half Painted. He then leaned back and stole a glance out the kitchen window, down the drive toward the shop just to be sure the truck did actually get washed.

Everything looked to be in order, so the water fight must have taken place on their way back to the shop to put things away. This was even more of an event when Carrie's youngest son, Axel's best friend Cory, came to visit. Their resemblance was so uncanny, that many people mistook them for twins. That's what both families referred to them as and equally traded them like custodial parental arrangements since the boys were almost always together. Brett really had his work cut out for him when The Twins took him on at the same time or wore him down tag teaming him, but he never gave in. Kat usually had to rearrange furniture and glue porcelain shards back together each time The Twins were in residence there.

Sam wondered for a scant second if Kat was engrossed enough for him to sneak a bite of a turnover while their sons were rolling around the floor like a bunch of heathens, but she was already putting an end to it.

"Alright you two, time to eat. You'll have to call it a draw. Now get out of those wet clothes and be back here in ten minutes, or I'm going to let your sister have first crack at the turnovers!"

They shimmied out of what they could without being indecent for the dash up the stairs, which was now of course a race and returned to put laundry in the washing machine before Kat could even get the salad dressings out. They were still laughing and poking at one another when they fell into their seats at the table with hair standing up everywhere from the hasty exit from their soaked t-shirts.

"Good night, you two look like a couple wild men from Borneo," Kat remarked, shaking her head.

Kasi-Ann was giggling in full agreement, her hand clapped over her mouth. Sam had already given his full attention to some papers he was briefly studying as he waited for everyone to gather at the table for the blessing and had barely noticed them. He set them aside as Kasi-Ann offered to do the honors. As soon as the *Amen* escaped her lips, the race to the kitchen to fix their plates began with Brett and Axel exploding out of their chairs.

"Okay, you two, that is about enough for tonight," Sam said chuckling, finally aware of their disheveled state.

"You don't have to make everything a competition. And if one of you steps on my toes in the middle of your foot race, my boot is gonna stomp all over your backsides," he said waving a fist at them, giving them his best Clint Eastwood squinting glare.

To which they paid absolutely no attention, knowing the playful sound of his voice and being presently captivated by the food before them. Otherwise, they were not above roping their father into their wrestling matches, whether he wished to be a willing participant or not.

They filled and stacked their plates and headed back to the long oak table, taking a seat to wait for everyone else. Sam was salting and peppering everything and shoving things around on his plate as he waited for Kasi-Ann who was still dishing up salad practically one leaf at a time, trying to find ones that the cucumber and tomato hadn't been in close proximity of, much less touched, heaven forbid. Kat considered her eating the greens alone was a small victory, but considered next time keeping some separate for her to speed the process along.

She could probably tell her that Camo Girl loved tomatoes, but there was no need to stretch the truth that far. She would probably come to like them as she got older anyways, so Kat left the Camo Girl card in her hand to be tossed during a real crisis. Besides, Kasi-Ann was keen enough to bring up the fact that Kat was not fond of tomatoes either and had already scooted the ones arriving in her serving of salad over onto Sam's plate.

Dinner miraculously concluded without any additional episodes of headlocks or pile driving. Kat watched Sam packing the papers he was perusing before dinner, retreating to his office instead of his giant slaying easy chair, with a cocked eyebrow of curiosity. He graciously shared the office with her, considering she was the resident accountant and bookkeeper, among other positions. The boys were already upstairs, pulling books out of backpacks, having officially waited until the very last minute to attend to their homework. Kasi-Ann was down the hall in her room humming, apparently busy at something.

Kat peeked into the study where Sam sat writing. It looked like an application of sorts, but she couldn't tell from the door.

"What's that, honey?" she asked.

"Well, something I've had in my back pocket for a little while now, and I'm just getting around to filling it out. It's an application for the Stillwater Mine."

"Really?" Kat asked, her voice trailing off.

Sam didn't look up from his paperwork. She wasn't even sure he had heard her; he was so intent on his writing.

"Do you know how to do a resume?" he asked, again without even glancing up. "Of course you do. Can you *help* me do one is what I meant," Sam asked, finally looking up at her standing in the doorway.

She entered the office, softly closing the door behind her.

"Where did this come from?" Kat inquired, feeling like it was an unexpected fly ball sailing deep into left field. "I thought the trucking was keeping things afloat financially. If I need to pick up something extra, honey, I can do that, it's not a problem …"

"Whoa, whoa, slow down, love. No, money isn't a problem. I just thought it might be wise to … investigate some other avenues you might say."

Her eyebrow was up again and practically to the rafters.

"Samuel Patterson, do you seriously expect me to believe for one minute that you are considering working for someone else after a lifetime of being your own boss?" she asked incredulously.

She had sounded a bit like his mother just then, and she knew it, but she was still too flabbergasted to make any apologies just yet. Not having to answer to anyone was something he had mentioned over and over that he loved about his lifestyle. Honestly, he worked harder than anyone she had ever known and could do well to learn to tell people *no* now and again. He already had the toughest boss on the planet—himself!

He leaned back in his chair and motioned her toward him. She sat down on his lap while he continued with his opening arguments, listening to words that just didn't quite seem to reach her ears, because presently, her own thoughts were drowning him out. She just couldn't imagine the thought of him making another huge lifestyle change. Living without cattle was an adjustment she still hadn't become accustomed to yet.

She was just thinking the other morning that it felt like snow and the first thing that came to mind was if it was deep enough and lasted very long, they would have to start feeding cows early. The realization of their state of *cowlessness* was still slow to sink in. It was like a death that she hadn't had time to properly mourn or have closure with. Sam was already moving on, practically jumping in with both feet.

When she finally started listening to him again, he was getting to the one reason that would strike a chord with her.

"And as I'm staring down the barrelhead of going back out on the road after such a great weekend with my family, I'm definitely motivated to look around at what other opportunities I have right here in my own backyard."

She heard that loud and clear. He was tired of being away from home. Her heart leapt. This was a decision she could not want enough for herself and her family for him to make, or let it press her to influence him, much less make for him. He had to come to this crossroads himself. If she had placed any demands on him, he would do his best to meet them, but deep down he would have resented her for it, much as he would have not wanted to or tried not to. She was never willing to take that chance but having him deciding to hang up trucking on his own was a horse of a whole different color, and right now she was happy enough to see rainbow-branded unicorns.

"Well, if you're sure you really want to do this, I'm behind you 100 percent as always. I know it would be something totally different than you've ever done, and I think that is sometimes exciting. Remember when I said good things always happen when we step out of the box? This could really be great, honey. I'm so proud of you for even considering this. You always take such good care of all of us, and this is just another testimony to your ability to adapt and overcome," she finished with tears beginning to well in her eyes.

"One bite at a time, I guess. I'll submit the application and see what happens. There's no guarantee they will even hire me. I hear they don't get in a very big hurry about filling the positions. In fact this application is just for a hiring pool, so my name goes into a hat with several others, and if they like what I—okay, *you* put on my resume, they will call me for an interview. If that goes well, then I go into a pool of other people that have been interviewed and accepted, and as positions become available, they start filling them on a first-come, first-served basis. So, it could be a whole bunch of hurry up and wait," Sam explained.

"Well then, it's a blessing that you don't need a job tomorrow, and we are taken care of until we decide to do something different," Kat offered.

"Exactly, we will have plenty of time to discuss any final decisions once we cross the other bridges. Until then, it's business as usual, as far as I'm concerned. Honestly, that's why I really didn't bring it up before now, but I'm glad we're both on the same page with it," Sam added.

"Oh, I swear I don't know how you do that! I get so excited about new things and then my two-year-old, redheaded impatience kicks in, and I want everything to happen now or know all the answers. You are so great at sitting back and waiting quietly," she went on, making her way to the door.

"Judas Priest!" she suddenly exclaimed, whirling back around. "Would you have even told me if I didn't see you filling out the application?" She wasn't really accusing him, but it would be just like him to think that there was no reason to get her all stirred up until he at least had an interview. She could certainly be counted on to get stirred up about things from time to time.

"Yes, dearest," he began slowly, trying to soothe her concerns. "I had planned to talk to you about it tonight after I had gotten the application filled out and the children went to bed. Remember me?" he asked, pointing his right index finger at his chest. "The guy sitting in my chair who asked you to help him with a resume? I wouldn't have handed it in without talking to you, and it certainly wouldn't have done me any good to turn it in incomplete without the resume. So yes, to point blankly answer your question, I had every intention of talking to you about it, and if you had been completely against it for whatever reason, I would have discarded the application and the idea altogether."

His eyes had clouded mildly with his own concern and sincerity as he stood looking down at her. He was reading her body language that had begun with a defensive, arms crossed stance. He had placed his hands on the sides of her shoulders as he had explained his reasoning. He stroked the sides of her arms as he spoke, slowly relaxing them down until they had come to rest at her side. He stepped back toward the mahogany desk and sat on top of it, pulling her toward him. He could now look her squarely in the eye, a position she certainly appreciated as a more equal and level playing field. He never dictated to her, but he fully understood that he could easily give that impression towering over her and usually sought a physical position that rendered them eye to eye.

He gently took hold of her hands and said, "Honey, you are my best friend, and I talk to you about everything. You always have such a unique and different perspective than I do, you help me see a full picture view of things. I appreciate the way you think, and your opinion means the world to me. I can't even imagine making a little decision without your input, much less a big one like this. You're the reason I don't go out in public with questionable wardrobe choices," he said teasingly. "Now, whether that information was solicited or not, is beside the point …" he continued, smiling, and winking playfully at her.

She finally cracked a smile. She still got a little dizzy every time he looked at her so intently, or winked at her and flashed that dazzling grin, but she knew every word was the gospel truth. He could be quite eloquent in his own genuine cowboy way, but he wasn't a silver-tongued devil. He never said things he didn't mean, nor did he sacrifice saying things that needed saying even if he didn't have pretty words to say it with. His brand of honesty spoke for itself and seldom ever needed words of any kind.

"Well, I suppose we should get to work then, eh? Resumes do not write themselves after all," she said taking a seat in front of the computer. "I believe I know just what will make yours stand out from the others. They'll be calling you for that interview before you know it," she said grinning at him.

They sat together for the next hour chronologically organizing his jack of all trades experience, condensing the pertinent information of types of equipment experience he possessed. It would have been easier to give them a list of things he didn't have experience with than what he did. Suffice it to say if it had four legs, he could ride it, if it had wheels and gears, he could drive it, regardless of how many.

On the rare occasion he came across something he hadn't driven before, five minutes time with the controls was about all he needed to obtain basic command of the vessel, another ten minutes would yield the finesse to make it fly if necessary. He was truly that good, and it was the success of the operation that reported this fact, not his mouth.

They had just finished printing their creation out and placed it in an envelope with the application when Kasi-Ann knocked and slowly walked into the office wearing pajamas and a pair of pink, fluffy bunny slippers.

"Mom, isn't it bedtime?"

"Good heavens," Kat muttered looking at an arm clock that read a quarter after 9:00 p.m. "Yes, young lady, it certainly is. Let's get you upstairs."

"How 'bout if I tuck you in, sis?" Sam asked as he picked her up and tossed her halfway over his shoulder. "You might be too big to do that next time I get home, and I don't want to miss my chance," he said as he reached up and tickled her middle with his free hand.

She squealed and flailed her legs nearly getting Kat in the nose with a flying foot. She walked around behind Sam and kissed the top of Kasi-Ann's head.

"Sweet dreams, beautiful girl. You are my greatest blessing. I love you like the air I breathe," Kat said softly.

Kasi-Ann lifted her head and reached out an arm to hug her mother. "I love you too, Mom. Good night."

"Alright, special delivery, one sack o' spuds, top floor, off we go," Sam said marching out of the office hauling Kasi-Ann up the stairs. She laughed all the way up in between professions about not being a spud.

Kat cleaned up the kitchen and packed a lunch for herself, then put some things together for Sam to take out on the road the next day. She started to make up the coffee pot and then her plans for revenge came flooding back. She placed a Bunn coffee filter in the basket and then put the coffee in. She heard Sam coming down the stairs, so she stopped at that point in the preparations and went into the bedroom to choose a uniform to set out for work the next day. She had already set his clean clothes out on the bed for him to put in his duffle bag. She sat down on the bed for a moment, staring at them, their significance suddenly overwhelming.

She really didn't want to think about him leaving again tomorrow, but it was taking center stage whether she wanted it to or not. She tried to force herself to think about the fact that this was the last month, and he would be home to stay soon. She tried to focus on the possible new job at the mine and that by this time next year maybe he wouldn't be trucking again. For all she knew, this could be the last fall run. It seemed impossible to believe such a complete change could take place, but she would never have envisioned the ranch without fences before the fire, and that was the current state of affairs, regardless of any amount of disbelief.

Change was inevitable she had told herself, but it was one thing to know it was coming and still another business altogether to see it manifest and to concede to change with it. Her inner redhead was having a control-freak temper tantrum about the free fall she felt herself in. She had to close her eyes and grip the edge of the bed to make the senseless reeling cease. When she opened them again, Sam was sitting down beside her.

"Howdy, ma'am. This seat taken?" he asked softly.

"Yes, my husband is sitting there," she answered, brushing a stray curl out of our face. "And he will probably not take too kindly to someone else taking his seat," she said quickly, trying to both be playful and hold herself together.

"You're right, I wouldn't," he said, realizing this was no time for their little game.

He read her like an open book.

"Honey, it's just a few more weeks and then it will be over, and I'll be home." She was staring at the comforter on the bed, tracing the quilted pattern with her finger. He gently tilted her chin up with his finger to look at him.

"I know. I'm just tired. Even though you have to leave, things will look better in the morning. They always do," Kat replied, a little surprised by her own cheerful outlook.

It certainly wasn't how she felt but having a poor mouth and complaining about the situation wasn't going to do anyone any good. On top of that, the last thing she needed to do was make her husband feel bad about what it took to make the living he took care of his family with.

Sam briefly hugged her and nodded, then slowly got up and began placing his clothes into the travel bag. When he finished, he set it on the floor by the bedroom door and went into the bathroom to brush his teeth and get ready for bed. She came in and hung her uniform on a hook on the back of the bathroom door and picked up her toothbrush that he had laid on the vanity for her. They stood side by side, staring at each other in the mirror with the buzz of electric toothbrushes whirring in stereo.

A few minutes later they crawled into bed.

"Ahhh, this is the second-best thing I've done all day," Sam said as he stretched out flat on his back, enjoying his last night for the week on a decent mattress.

"And what was the best?" She asked smiling, right on cue, as though she didn't know the answer to the question she put to him every time he made that remark.

"Waking up next to you," he answered, reaching over to hold her hand.

He gently tugged on it, asking her to come lay on his chest. She rolled over and laid her head down with her left cheek on his chest, inhaling his familiar scent, and sighed. *It's only a few more weeks,* she told herself again. Sam reached up to move a couple of her curls that were now tickling his face and then settled into what was one of his favorite places on the planet. She so naturally gravitated to the same exact spot every time that he teased her about wearing the hair off the left side of his chest.

It wasn't particularly true as he wasn't given much body hair to begin with, but for whatever reason there was considerably less hair that grew on the left side of both his chest and abdomen. There had been more than one occasion that she had awakened in the middle of the night, realizing that she had fallen asleep there and clearly had been drooling all over him for a considerable expanse of time. She would mop up the puddle and flop over with him barely aware of any of it, but he seized the opportunity to tease her about rubbing too hard, taking the hair right off him.

Kat suddenly remembered her unfinished plans and sat up with a start. "I'll be right back, she said, and jumped down off the bed heading for the kitchen.

She flipped on the light and began rummaging in what they called the junk drawer for some electrical tape. She was almost certain that he would not get out of bed to see what she was up to as comfortable as he had said he was, but she still tried to work quickly. If she got busted in the middle of her plan, it would certainly foil her revenge. She quickly went over to the sink, unraveling a length of the tape, d wrapping it around the depressed black handle of the sprayer on the right side of the Moen faucet. The tape was a darker black than that of the handle, but in the low light of the kitchen window lamp at 4:00 a.m., it would be virtually undetectable. She put the roll of tape back in the drawer and jumped back into bed.

Sam had obviously already drifted off for a moment while she was in the kitchen and really had no idea how long she had been gone. He asked what she was doing, and she simply answered that she forgot to put the coffee in the coffeemaker so it would be ready for him in the morning. She would get up with him so they could visit and have coffee together for a little while before he left.

The alarm seemed like it sounded the minute she closed her eyes. She clearly had been tired enough that she hadn't moved a muscle, or the night really was only forty-five seconds long; she couldn't decide for sure. She laid there thinking she wanted to hit the snooze, but the alarm was on the bedside table on Sam's side of the bed and he was already in the bathroom washing up. She decided to close her eyes for a few more minutes until he came out then she would face the day.

Sam exited the bathroom, the light shining right on the bed where Kat lay face down in her pillow, unmoving, red curls splayed out like a welcome mat. He shook his head and began getting dressed, waiting for her to give any impression that she had a pulse. When she didn't, he decided he would go make some coffee to tempt her out of her cocoon. He tossed his shirt back onto the bed and zipped up his pants, figuring to finish the job of dressing with a hot cup of inspiration to motivate himself.

He reached up above the coffee pot to the small lamp by the window and clicked it on. He thought he remembered Kat saying something about getting the coffeepot ready but pulled the basket out and checked to be sure. It had a fresh new liner and coffee inside, so he flipped the handle of the faucet on and cranked it over toward the left for cold water to fill the carafe. Instantly, an icy shower from the sprayer came out of nowhere, hitting him smack in his bare chest. He jumped back gasping and sputtering at the initial shock and then realized that it wasn't stopping. He let out a bellow as he waded in close enough to reach the handle and shoved it down, finally halting the frigid version of Old Faithful that was going off in their kitchen.

Kat was suddenly awake and bounded out of bed as she remembered what he was reacting to.

She ran to the bedroom door and pulled it open and hollered, "*Gotcha!*" bursting into laughter.

"Why you little ..." Sam exclaimed, not even able to come up with a suitable insult, technically knowing he was getting his due. He was not above playing dirty, however, and he grabbed the sprayer and flipped the water back on, getting her sufficiently soaked before she could manage a squealing retreat behind the door. He dropped the sprayer into the sink and turned the water off, chasing her into the bedroom. He caught her just as she was trying to get through the bathroom door. They were both laughing, dripping wet and delightfully wide awake for 4:10 a.m.

"Our sons would be so proud," Kat finally said between bouts of giggles. "I'm sure we've stirred the whole house up by now."

"Oh, I seriously doubt that. Some days I think you could burn it down around them and they wouldn't notice," Sam offered. "I do believe I am going to need a different pair of pants. I don't think I'm terribly interested in running the Fort Morgan 500 in soggy Wranglers."

"Aww, where did you double park your sense of adventure, Patterson—or did you leave it in your other pants?" she taunted.

"Woman, you are seriously asking for it," he said, charging at her. He grabbed her up and tossed her up onto the bed and proceeded to tickle her until she couldn't even speak.

After some time, she was finally able to sufficiently catch her breath from wailing and thrashing, but she got up off the bed and still had to work at gathering her wits. He was just setting out dry clothes when she casually mentioned on her way to the kitchen that she was obviously going to have to make the coffee herself this morning since he was clearly incapable of doing much more than making puddles.

That comment landed her squarely in the shower. She hadn't even heard him coming. She heard the shower turn on in the bathroom and figured Sam decided on a full run through the rain room, considering he was already half soaked. She removed the electrical tape from the sprayer and started the coffee, She was standing in the kitchen looking down the drive at Half Painted parked under the power pole security light in front of the shop. He had snuck up behind her like a thief in the night, scooped her up in one swoop and hauled her into the bathroom.

"I'll give you puddles, woman," he said, laughing as he pulled the curtain back and plopped her in the shower, bathrobe and all. There had been no use in fighting and she was truthfully a little played out from having been nearly tickled to the brink of peeing her pants earlier. She stood there laughing in what was at least warm water, looking up at him. He was thoroughly satisfied.

He then stepped in with her, closed the curtain, lifted her up in a big bear hug and said, "*Gotcha!*"

She vowed to herself never again to try to beat the man at his own game. Clearly, he had no scruples and essentially no rules. The last time she had tried the ice water stunt on him while he was in the shower, he burst out of there in nothing but his all-togethers and chased her not only out of the bedroom, but out of the house and into the driveway, scaring an unsuspecting UPS man half to death. He was brand new and had been properly pleased with himself for finding their rural address on the first try, though he never did wear that same pleasant smile ever again honestly. After that he looked as nervous as a long-tailed cat in a room full of rocking chairs. In fact, whenever he dropped off packages, he practically tossed them to the porch from the gate fifteen feet away and dashed back to the truck, never looking at anything but the ground.

This was at least a time period before the arrival of children, but it should have dawned on her then, he would go to any length to win, and this was not a battleground for the faint of heart—so says the blushing bride of Samuel Patterson and one permanently scarred postal employee.

## CHAPTER 12

# A Christmas Miracle?

November made a blustering entrance with some freezing rain that was followed up by a week-long blizzard. It left the roads covered in inch-thick ice and several feet of snow on the ground. Sam ended up having a couple near misses on the icy roads that he elected to leave between him and God, because his wife would have had him committed right next to her had she been in possession of the full details.

The last one involved a narrow bridge at the bottom of a long sloping hill in which multiple cars had lost control in front of him. They were bouncing off the sides of the bridge and guard rail, there was no way he was going to get that truck shut down in time to avoid a collision. Every time he touched the brakes, he could feel the trailer start to swim. Harboring the singular thought that he would surely kill someone on impact, he braced himself with both hands on the wheel. He knew he never once closed his eyes, but he couldn't tell you why, beyond the mercy of God, that he didn't hit any of those cars. There couldn't have been more than an inch in some places. It had felt like he passed between them in slow motion, watching them sliding just beyond the grill of the truck and out of harm's way.

When he made it past all of them and far enough out of the way to pull over, he eased off the road and sat there shaking like a leaf for several minutes. Before long, he even had to get out of the truck and walk around to try to clear his head. He made several laps around Half Painted, looking for even a tiny scratch that would indicate he had touched anything or anyone else, but came up with nothing. It was like God had reached down with both hands and guided him through, bringing all of them out unscathed.

He was a great driver with many years of experience, but he knew better than to try to take credit for this because it simply shouldn't have happened. Someone should be dead. He might have survived the crash because his vehicle won the size contest, but even that was no guarantee. Everyone else would have undoubtedly perished. He shuddered as he thought of the other drivers and families in their cars. He looked toward the heavens, knowing he had witnessed and experienced a great demonstration of mercy.

He had arrived home to stay a couple weeks before the Thanksgiving holiday with more reasons to be grateful than he could possibly count. December had snuck in the back door while nobody was looking, and all were counting down the days until Christmas.

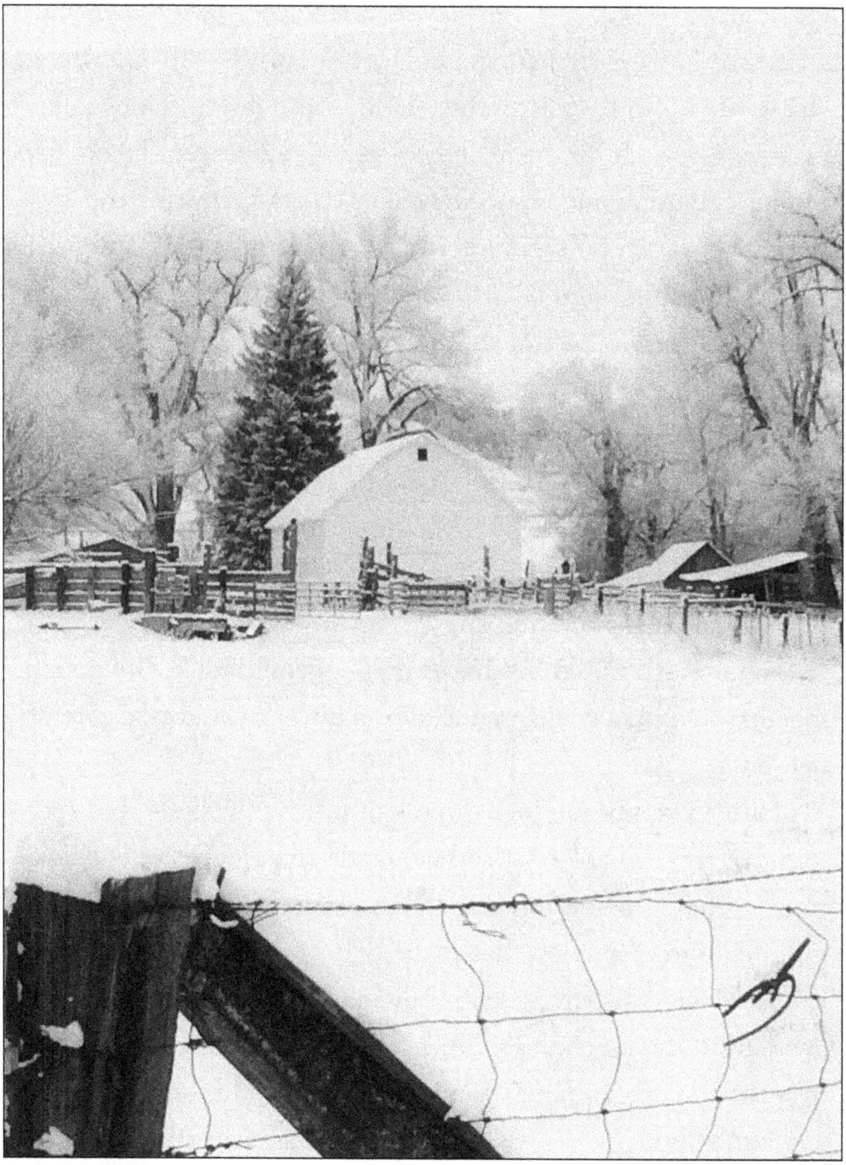

Kasi-Ann was sitting at the dining room table after school, well into her third draft of a letter to Santa. The crumpled, rejected first and second versions were laying on the floor behind her chair where she had tossed them in mild frustration. As with everything, she wanted it to be perfect, but she was also facing the deadline of having it ready for the mail the next morning, according to her mother. Figuring out what she wanted to ask for wasn't the only issue; there was also the matter of penmanship and neatness. If she could get her pen to behave and be cooperative, this would certainly expedite the process. So far it had leaked great blue ink blobs all over versions one and two and she was wiping it with a tissue again before she could continue with round three.

The other issue at hand was that today was the day she and her mother were making Christmas cookies. She was distracted because this was her favorite Christmas tradition. She wasn't particularly pleased about missing out on any of it, even for a letter to Santa. Kat assured her however, they could make the dough together and then while it chilled for a bit, she could take care of her letter.

Letter attempt number three had just received another spattering of small ink blobs as she shook the pen that just one second prior didn't provide any ink at all for writing purposes. She groaned and crumpled that piece of paper, tossing it over her head and onto the floor with the others. She scooted her chair back away from the table and padded off down the hall to the office to retrieve more supplies. Sam looked up from his office chair as she came through the door frowning. He was busy rifling through their file cabinets, looking for the most recent brand inspections on the horses.

## A Christmas Miracle?

"Why the scowl, kiddo?" Sam asked, failing to hide the smile from his own face. She could tell her own stories without bothering with words for the expressions that her face displayed.

"Stupid pen keeps ruining my letter," she stated with the conviction of both a judge and jury combined.

She went to the desk drawer containing printer paper and removed a sheet and then closed it again. She paused a moment and reopened it, taking another sheet just in case she should have any issues during the next attempt.

Sam held out his pen holder toward her so she could select a different pen. She reached up showing off a hand blotched with blue ink spots everywhere and chose a bright yellow Yellowstone Bank pen. Sam examined her hand briefly and then asked where the other pen was.

"Garbage," she answered flatly, her face displaying her utter disgust. There was clearly no pity for this pen gone bad. She was on a mission to finish her letter, so without any further discussion, she took her leave from the office and headed back to the dining room table.

She only had one thing she could think of to ask for and that was a .22 long rifle. She knew this was too extravagant for a Santa letter so needed to think of something else, but it was her heart's true desire. She had paid her dues on the .22 single shot Cricket that each of the Patterson brood had started with and was now setting her sights—literally—on her own gun. She imagined Camo Girl had a whole gun safe filled with firearms like her dad. She was excited about starting her own collection.

She would be grateful for any model or design it came by, but if she were to be able to pick the exact one, it would be the pink Muddy Girl design. She had come to love shooting from helping to change irrigation water with her brothers, who always had a gun strapped to the rack of the quad. It was never known when one would have to do battle with a snake, skunk or ill-tempered badger lurking in the tall grass of the hay fields and simply best to always have a little fire power on hand.

After expressing interest in shooting, Brett and Sam got out the Cricket, cleaned and oiled it up and began instructing her in firearm safety and basic operation. They were both equally impressed with her attention and willingness to learn, but it was her natural ability and growing marksmanship that brought the smiles of pride to their faces. Kat quietly patted her own back, thinking that this little apple hadn't fallen far from the tree, as she was no slouch with a firearm either.

Kasi-Ann saw her mother open the fridge and reach in to poke the sugar cookie dough, testing it for firmness. She looked down at her page that was still empty and knew it was time to get the job done, ink blobs or not.

She began with a sincere *Dear Santa*, as though she knew him personally, and without meaning to sound presumptuous, truly felt as though she did. She had an imagination almost as vivid as Nana Posie, who loved to tell Christmas stories in particular. The way she described St. Nick from top to bottom, one couldn't help but feel like they had just sat on his jolly lap and could smell the peppermint of the candy canes in his pocket.

She continued with well wishes for Mrs. Clause, all of the elves and reindeer, concluding her pleasantries with hopes for good weather for flying on Christmas Eve. Then she addressed the heart of the matter, but her pen came to a dead halt, the remaining page as blank as her mind that sought to produce an idea for a gift request. She tapped her pen lightly on the paper as they thought. Still nothing materialized.

She didn't have any real interest in most girly things, so the best she was going to do on short notice was a game of some kind. She expressed how she loved to play games with her family and that a new game they could all play together would be wonderful. She closed with a big blue heart and *Love, Kasi-Ann,* then folded it neatly, placing it in the envelope her mother had provided her with earlier. She carefully put *SANTA, North Pole* on the front of the long, white envelope and sealed it. It felt like a giant weight was lifted from her shoulders to have the task completed, as she took it to her mother in the kitchen. Kat placed it with a stack of bills, letters and Christmas cards that would be dropped off at the post office when they went to town later that afternoon.

"Okay, pretty girl, go poke that dough and see if it's ready to become the most amazing Christmas cookies the world has ever seen!" Kat told Kasi-Ann.

She already knew it was ready; she merely wanted her to think it was just now firm enough and that she hadn't kept her waiting with her letter writing. For a young girl, she was very sensitive to other people's needs and how her own words and actions affected people. Kat fervently hoped that she went out and infected the world with this quality of kindness it was in such desperate need of.

"It's ready!" Kasi-Ann exclaimed as she grabbed the ball of dough wrapped in wax paper out of the refrigerator. They always had music playing whenever they worked together in the kitchen and that was Kasi-Ann's next exclamation. "We need tunes, Mom!"

"You're right! This kitchen needs some Christmas music. Ya can't bake Christmas cookies without Christmas music, it's un-American!" Kat qualified.

"Amen!" Kasi-Ann concurred, laughing.

"Is that really a rule?" Sam asked, smirking as he came from the office into the kitchen, brand inspections in hand. "I could swear I've had mute Christmas cookies before—never sang a single note, not one of them," he added looking quite proud of himself for thinking of something so clever to say.

"No, Dad, the cookies don't sing or make the music," Kasi-Ann instructed, completely crushing his attempt at humor. "The radio makes the music while we make the cookies."

Her eyes brightened with a new realization.

"But if a cookie was ever going to sing, I bet it would be a gingerbread man! And the voice would probably be deep and low like the man who sings the Grinch song," she followed.

Sam reached out and ruffled Kasi-Ann's hair. "I don't know where you come up with your ideas, but that's pretty funny stuff, sis."

"Well, I got a kick out of your notion about mute cookies, honey," Kat said, patting Sam on the back gently. "I'm sure if we put our minds to it, we can make some extra-special Christmas cookies this year. We'll have those bells ringing and angels singing in no time, right, Kasi?" Kat asked her cookie co-pilot.

"Right!" Kasi-Ann chimed in. "Let's get to work!"

Sam kissed Kat on the cheek and said he would get out of their hair and leave them to it. He put on his coat and went out the door toward the barn to file a copy of the current brand inspections in the tack room for quick retrieval. His cell phone was buzzing and ringing in his shirt pocket a moment later.

"Hello?"

"Good morning, is this Sam Patterson?" the caller's singsong voice inquired.

"Yep, you got him, what can I do for ya?" he answered back in his own usual cheerful manner.

"Sam, this is Ashley from HR at Stillwater Mining Company. I'm calling to set you up for an interview for the position you applied for. Do you have a day or time this week that would work well for you?"

"Well, I guess about any time would work for me. I'm pretty flexible," Sam answered, his mind beginning to swim a little. This was unexpectedly fast, but he had already made up his mind that he was going to at least check it out in person, and the opportunity was now presenting itself.

"Well how about tomorrow at 9:00 a.m.?" Ashley offered.

"That sounds great. Where should I go?" Sam asked, realizing he had absolutely no idea whether the interviews were conducted onsite or in town at the HR office.

"You will be going directly out to the mine site so you can have an underground tour and get a feel for where you will be working, and the equipment and so forth." she said. Do you know how to get there?"

"Yes, ma'am, I do. I will be there at 9:00 a.m. sharp."

"Wonderful, we'll see you in the morning, Sam. Goodbye."

"Thanks. Goodbye."

Sam heard the line go dead and closed the screen on his phone to put it in his shirt pocket. He knew he should turn right around and go right back to the house and tell Kat, but she was going to be up to her elbows in cookie dough for a couple more hours, and God's truth, he needed a little time for all of this to sink in. It was just an interview, but it was the first step toward getting a job up there, and it already felt like it was happening faster than he might be completely comfortable with. He tried to push it out of his mind as he filed the brand inspections, but a host of what-if scenarios and questions kept stealing their way back into his central train of thought.

At last, he decided he wasn't going to know much more until after the interview, and for a moment, caught a glimpse of Kat's impatience when she wanted questions answered. He was surprised at himself that even tomorrow morning seemed like too long to wait for them and thought for a moment he might have a conversation with Kat about her impatient spirit rubbing off on him. On second thought, he quickly discarded the notion in favor of having sense enough not to poke the bear. Even the little cinnamon bears can get surprisingly hot after all.

In point of fact, the conversation regarding the interview would also be put on a back burner at least until tomorrow evening. She would be bursting with questions if he told her about it tonight, but then neither of them would sleep—her, because she would be awake wondering ten million different things—and him, because she would be compelled to share at least a half million of the wonderings out loud with him. He would be just getting back to town by the time she went to lunch and thought to maybe stop in surprise her with a short visit and a treat from the local bakery as a peace offering for not having told her sooner. He would give her the full details then, including the answers to his own burning questions, whatever they may be.

He had stared into space, trying not to think about it all through dinner. He even absentmindedly plowed through three heavily frosted sugar cookies for dessert, consumed by thoughts about not thinking about it. Kat asked twice what the matter was, to which he responded he was just tired. He had been home a few weeks now, but still he had erratic sleep patterns that would keep him up half the night one night and lay him out cold shortly after Kasi-Ann went to bed the next.

He barely slept a wink that night and was beginning to believe it was penance for his decision to not tell Kat about the interview, but the bellyache of two additional cookies was vying for enough attention that he placed equal blame there as well. After she left for work, he was sitting at the dining room table having coffee, his conscience would no longer let him be. He had to tell her or risk running mad from the whispering voices in his head. He figured he'd give her another thirty minutes to get to work safely and then send her a text to let her know he was going up to the mine this morning.

He showered and dressed, noting that the eyes gazing back at him from his reflection were dry and red from being overtired as he brushed his teeth. He reached into the vanity drawer for some Visine, giving each eye a healthy flush. The last thing he needed was to present for an interview, looking like he was in danger of bleeding to death from his eye sockets. Luckily, they had cleared by the time he was getting into the pickup to leave.

He still hadn't gotten a reply from Kat, but he figured she might not get a chance to check messages until later in the morning. That was probably fortuitous as she would be blowing up his phone with all the questions he had intended to dodge the night before. The more he thought about it, it might also distract her from her work and that wasn't exactly good either. *Well, what's done is done*, he thought to himself. There wasn't much else he could do about it now. He would likely be out of phone service by the time she noticed the message and be bombarded by several texts by the time he got back down off the mountain. He fidgeted uncomfortably in his seat at that thought and considered a stop by the floral shop along with the bakery might not hurt either.

The longer he drove, the faster he went. He decided it would be wise to set the cruise control about the second time he realized his foot was getting heavy. He was trying to organize his thoughts and questions as well as stay in tune to watching the road. Multitasking didn't seem to be his forte today. It occurred to him then that he might be just a little bit nervous. He couldn't remember the last time he had gone to a formal interview. It was all too possible that he had *never* been to one. All of the employment prior to being fully self-employed were ranch jobs in and out of high school. After that, there was a short stint of following the buckaroo trail where everything he owned was bought, paid for and fit in the camper shell of a baby blue Chevy pickup. He had the whole world at his feet with everything out front from the view of a windshield beckoning him to explore, and he didn't owe it a dime.

What he didn't see of the world through the glass of that old Chevy, he saw from behind the wheel of a semi. He had driven with his father a short time and then bought his own truck and set out to be a self-made man. It had been that way from that day to this one. A job change would now mean he would be "working for the man," and while he didn't quite like the sound of that, he still found he was curious enough to have applied and accepted the opportunity for an interview. He even admitted that if he truly was nervous about it, it was probably more because he wanted it more than he had expected, not because he wasn't sure if he could do it. There wasn't anything in his mind that he couldn't do if he set out to do it. The competition he ran against was only ever himself, pressing harder to achieve more today than yesterday, whether it was one more load, or even just one more mile.

## A Christmas Miracle?

Shortly after entering onto mine property, he pulled up to the guard shack and stated the reason for his visit, to which the guard directed him to the adjacent parking lot and main entrance. *Well, here we go,* he thought as he parked the pickup and began walking toward the door. A bright and cheery face met him at the door.

"Good morning, Sam. I'm Ashley. I'm glad you could make it," she said with a friendly smile.

An hour and a half later, he returned to his pickup and proceeded to make his way back to town. It had all gone extremely well, and he felt fairly certain that they would be adding his name to the hiring pool.

Twenty minutes later, a single text message from Kat chimed in on his phone. He pulled off the road for a moment, needing to take off his coat anyway. He was so busy thinking about the course of events of the interview and tour that he climbed in the pickup with his heavy coat still on. He was normally so hot blooded he could sweat in the shower, so wearing a coat in the cab of a vehicle was practically intolerable. He was about to die of heat exhaustion even with the heater off and the window down, so when the message sounded, he added it to the need of getting his coat off to produce enough inclination to pull over and stop for a moment. He was more than a little bent on getting to town, but the coat simply had to go, and he needed to at least see what Kat's message sent.

"Oh Sam, that's wonderful news! Let me know how it goes. Good luck, honey. Love you," the single message read.

He was mildly shocked that the message wasn't riddled with questions and that there was only one message, but that could be for any number of reasons. She could be busy with patients or other duties at work too. He sent her back a message that it had all gone well and that he would be stopping by for lunch if she was available.

He then remembered lunch time was coming up quickly and decided to call an order in for them while he was still sitting still. He spoke briefly with the restaurant owner who said he was going to bring lunch over for Daisy and offered to deliver lunch to her as well when he picked up their order. He hung up and got back on the road, now able to make his first stop in town at the bakery. They made a specialty cream cheese lemon muffin that Kat adored, so that was a must-have item, along with something chocolate for the rest of the ladies in the office. If he was going for atonement, it surely wouldn't hurt to have her colleagues singing his praises a little. They were just boxing up his items when Kat sent a text back that she would be free for lunch in the next fifteen minutes. He replied he would be there by then and to let Daisy know he was dropping off her lunch as well.

As he pulled into the back parking lot of the clinic, Kat and Daisy were coming out of the employee entrance. Daisy thanked him for the delivery service as he handed her the square Styrofoam container with a big heart drawn on top in red pen ink.

"Awww. Look what he put on there; he is just so sweet," Daisy drawled out.

The bite of the December wind that was picking up, swirling snow around. The girls silenced that sentiment quickly, however.

"Dang! Okay, ya'll can stay out here n' catch your death if ya want, but I'm taking this back inside," she said as she spun on her heel and headed back to the clinic with her food. "Thanks, Sam!" she hollered over her shoulder.

Kat climbed up into the pickup where it was nice and warm and immediately smelled her muffin. Her eyes lit up and she turned and looked in the back seat, seeing the pink bakery box nestled back there with his discarded coat.

"What's all this, then?" she asked brightly.

"Oh, just feeling good about the interview and wanted to come celebrate a little with you," Sam said.

"Well, I was sure surprised when I got your message about the interview. From the time I got it and the time you said the appointment was, I figured you would already be out of service on your way up there. I couldn't help it, though. I said a prayer that it would go well and then sent you a message anyway, knowing you wouldn't see it until you were done, silly as that is. Then I ran around the rest of the morning like a chicken with my head cut off; we were so busy," she said crossing her eyes. "I didn't even have a chance to check my messages again until right when you sent me the message about bringing lunch. I was very excited about that too. Thank you, honey; this is a wonderful treat! Oh, I'm so happy to see you and so happy *for* you! When do you think you will hear from them?" she asked, finishing the 100 mile-per-hour ramble, Kasi-Ann style, as if Sam didn't already know the poor child came by it honestly.

"Well, sounds like they were happy with my interview as well, and I am going into the pool. There are a couple more people ahead of me, but it even sounds like they have some positions opening up soon that they will be filling. I guess there's no real way to tell how long it will take to get to my place in the lineup, but at least I know I'm hired if we choose to accept it."

"Oh, of course you are, they'd be silly not to put an asset like you to work for them. Good heavens, you've probably driven more miles in reverse than the whole crew combined has driven forward! I really think you should do it, honey. Why not? It's not like you have anything to lose, honestly. You're always going to have the skill set and experience for ranching and trucking, and think of what other equipment you might get to learn to operate," she said, her Eskimo ice-selling sales pitch gaining momentum. "Learning something new is always good and challenges wake up our potential. Besides, you're great at everything!" she said waving a "nothing to worry about" hand at him.

"Well, I guess we'll cross that bridge when we get that phone call. In the meantime, eat your lunch, babe. You'll have to go back in soon and you haven't eaten yet," he said, sounding more like a father than a husband.

She rolled her eyes at his steadfast modesty and opened her to-go box to find a beautiful chef salad. In her excitement over the interview and the news about the new job, she too felt it was a little celebration.

"I'm taking my cues from you today, Sam, and I'm having my dessert first. We only get one trip around, right?" she asked, smiling, as she handed him his own advice. "I'm having my muffin first," she said closing her salad container and reaching for the bakery box.

She unwrapped the lemon muffin and inhaled its creamy citrus scent. It made her think of summer, which was a far cry from what was happening outside her window just then, but that made it all the sweeter. She took a bite, thinking about what Daisy had said about David sending her lunch with a cute heart on it, and she couldn't help but feel like a spoiled brat. Sam was celebrating some good news, and he had made the effort to bring *her* not only lunch, but her favorite treat. His goodness had not even stopped there, but he thought to bring extras for Daisy and their coworkers as well.

"Sam, thank you for being so thoughtful. I appreciate this visit and that you were so excited to tell me your news. Having you bring us lunch and all the extra goodies was a wonderful bonus to the great company," she finished beaming at him.

Suddenly he felt like Pete slinking back from the chicken coop, guilt ridden and questioning himself over his conduct. The first thing on her mind when she heard about the interview was to send him a good luck message even when she knew he wouldn't see it until after it was all said and done. She had sent up a prayer on his behalf along with the good wishes and now was full of encouragement.

She was thrilled to hear his news, simply because she knew he was happy. She wasn't playing twenty questions over the situation. She was gratefully gushing thanks and praise all over him for a stupid salad and a lemon muffin. He spied the clock on the radio that indicated she only had about ten more minutes before she had to go back in and knew it wasn't quite long enough for him to make a very good apology, but he wasn't going to feel right about not saying something. He had deliberately not told her about the interview after professing that he shared everything with her and always valued her opinion.

"You're welcome, though I have something to tell you about that I'm not very proud of," he said staring at the Ford emblem in the center of the steering wheel.

"Oh?" Kat inquired softly, looking concerned at the prospect of bad news.

"Yeah, I knew about the interview yesterday," he said, getting right to the heart of the matter. "They called to schedule it while you were making cookies. At first I didn't want to bother you with it while you were busy, but then I think I wanted a little time to wrap my own head around it, I guess. I spent a long time trying to figure out what questions I might want to ask and trying to mentally prepare for whatever they were going to ask of me. You always get so excited about this kind of stuff. I was afraid if I told you, it might be more of a distraction, and we'd be up all night because you would have tons of questions about stuff that I wouldn't be able to answer yet, so I just didn't say anything. To be honest that decision went and bit me right square in the set-upon, because I'm the one who didn't sleep last night for all the questions swirling around in my head. I didn't have answers for any of those ones either, now that I think about it. I guess I'm trying to say I'm sorry. It sure enough feels like a lie not telling you," he said, ending his voluntary confession, never having taken his eyes off the steering wheel.

Kat had relaxed the second he mentioned the interview. For a moment he had thought there was some other big decision or problem that she needed to know about, but she was polite enough to let him finish airing his concerns thoroughly. Once he finally arrived at the apology portion of the exercise, sounding properly contrite at that, she decided to let him off the hook.

"I know, Sam, but thank you for telling me. For what it's worth, I know I can be a handful when I'm on about something," she said, owning her known shortcomings.

"Wait. What? What do you mean you know," he asked genuinely bewildered.

"I talked to the lady from HR when she called the house, looking for you. Ashley, wasn't it? Anyway, she said they wanted to schedule you for an interview so I asked her to call you on your cell phone because you were out in the shop. I didn't know what you had up your sleeve for things to do over the next couple days.

## A Christmas Miracle?

When you didn't say anything about it and you looked so distant and deep in thought during dinner, I figured you needed a little time to mull it all over. That's why I didn't ask you or say anything else about it. I didn't want to pester you," she replied.

"For the love of Christmas, woman, I've been beside myself for the past twelve hours because I didn't tell you and all this time you already knew?!" he asked exasperated. "Aaahhgh, you're killing me!" he groaned.

Kat laughed, realizing that he had brought her lunch and treats to butter her up for this apology that was essentially unnecessary, then burst into a fit of hysteria complete with a couple inelegant snorts as she tried to regain her oxygen supply. That was proving to be a feat, as every time she looked at the disgusted expression he bore, she would relapse into another round of side-stitching chortling.

Sam had kept his eye on the clock while his wife was indisposed for the course of her temporary insanity. At the point when Daisy opened the back door of the clinic and peeked out to see what was keeping Kat, Sam got out of the driver's seat, opened the back door of the crew cab to retrieve the bakery box and proceeded around to Kat's door. She was still attempting to come up for air when he opened the door, and she came tumbling out at him. He caught her enough to assist her in landing on her feet and the sudden change in location seemed to have finally commanded her undivided attention.

Sam handed her the bakery box, stacking her salad on top of it and said, "You're late; you best be getting back inside."

"Oh, my goodness, I totally lost track of the time," she said, working hard to hold back some residual snickering. "Ok, thanks, honey; I'll see you at home."

He walked her to the back door and opened it up for her since her hands were full and then said, "Yep, have a good afternoon." He gave her a chaste kiss on the cheek and then turned to leave. He could hear her burst out laughing with renewed enthusiasm behind the door as he walked back to the pickup shaking his head.

*I swear if I live to be 100, I will never figure that woman out,* he thought to himself as he drove out of the parking lot. He knew better than to linger any longer on the topic because the perfectionist in him would want to tear it apart, analyze and reanalyze what had just happened, searching for even a shred of logic or some other concept that would attempt to make a lick of sense. Three mind-numbing days later, he would still have no more insight or answers than he had at this very moment, so it was best off to just accept that he would never unravel this little redheaded mystery. Not only that, but after Kat ceased her insufferable laughter, she would have completely moved on, barely seeing fit to give the occurrence a second thought, much less feeling it necessary to yield any effort toward a cross examination of it.

He needed to busy his hands and occupy his mind elsewhere. He pulled into the drive and parked the pickup under the open-faced shed next to the shop, thinking he would go work on Kat's Christmas present. Christmas was only a week away, and while he had drafted a full schematic in his head, he was yet to even start gathering up the parts for the project.

As he went to open the shop door, he was only able to move the door a few inches before it came to a halt against something heavy.

"Who goes there?" boomed out in Brett's voice.

"It's me," Sam answered impatiently.

"Me who?" Axel's voice inquired this time, with an air of humor Sam couldn't possibly appreciate today.

## A Christmas Miracle?

"Oh, for the love of ... open the door!" Sam insisted.

"Not a chance. You know the rules, Dad. You can't just go barging into the shop this time of year; it ruins surprises," Brett followed.

"*You* made the rules, Dad," Kasi-Ann chimed in.

It *was* Sam's rule. As the boys got old enough to use more tools and equipment, they would all find themselves vying for time and access to the shop and inadvertently spoiling the fun by revealing their gift ideas when someone unexpectedly walked in to retrieve items to work with. From November 1st after the drawing of names on Halloween, to December 24th, everyone was to knock before entering and announce themselves so gifts in progress could be covered, removed from view or from the entire premises if necessary, prior to entry.

Failure to comply would render the passing of the sentence of a minimum of fifty, maximum of 150, lashings with a wet noodle or any/all other forms of allotted punishments, as deemed suitable by the presiding Honorable Judge Patterson. Kasi-Ann, having been called for multiple appearances in the Court of Mom, soon found it was simply easier to knock on any door before entering. It wasn't so much of a problem that she saw someone else's gift in the making, it was her honest, but bucket-sized mouth, that accidentally brought it up in conversation later.

Disgruntled, Sam looked at his watch, thinking it was early for the kids to be home, but then he remembered they had an early out for teacher's meetings and were obviously taking advantage of the time to work on their gifts. He also knew Brett had drawn his name this year, so there was no point in trying to get into the shop for now, since he was obviously busy working in there for the time being. He needed to go shopping in some junk piles and other miscellaneous "hidey-holes" for the pieces he needed anyway, so he could do that first. Getting everything gathered up and started this early was out of character for him anyway. Christmas Eve day was usually his cue to get it together, like he somehow performed better under pressure. At this point, he would argue that it would be the only time he could get into the shop. Kat, of course, was done with her gift two weeks ago.

He had a couple of particular items he was on the hunt for and thought he could walk right to them, but this was not proving to be the case. He always said he had one very special hidey-hole that he put everything he wanted to find right away. Trouble was, he had absolutely no idea where that one was when he needed the stuff back out of it. He even accused it of magically changing locations somehow. It was, after all, a much better story than simply not remembering where the dickens he put things. He was now beginning to surmise that the items in question were in said hidey-hole.

He always had a couple of gift ideas in mind, so if one failed, he had a plan B, but he really did want to proceed with his original plan. He was going to make her a metal boot rack out of angle iron and old horseshoes because she was forever complaining about tripping over all the boots on the mud room floor. The three-tiered rack would house twelve pairs of boots, effectively clearing up the excess that were constantly scattered about. It would be painted black to match the horseshoe coat and hat hooks already adorning the mudroom wall. Now if he could just lay his hands on the last few pieces of angle iron and rebar he needed.

In the shop, Brett was steady at work on a blade he was fashioning out of an old horseshoe rasp. It would be a small fleshing blade perfect for his father's hunting pack, complete with a custom made, basket stamped, leather sheath bound in rawhide. He was even able to do some of the work at school in shop class for credit in a custom metal project category, which had helped keep his gift out of sight at home thus far. He had spent the last hour swearing Kasi-Ann to secrecy, convincing her that the Court of Big Brother was a far cry from the Court of Mom.

Axel was already done with Kasi-Ann's gift, which was providence since like most pesky little sisters, she was always intent on being in their hip pockets. He had constructed a metal cowboy stand to hold her Kindle reader. His body was a tall, slender, rectangular piece of metal with a giant horseshoe for both upper and lower limbs, repurposed from the shire horses' old shoes. The top one was upside down with a bend in both sides to make the forward outstretched arms that held the kindle. In the center of the top shoe, a head was welded on. It bore a round washer with a large nut on top to fashion the cowboy's hat, similar to Chase's flat-top style. Axel had even trimmed down a small horseshoe nail and added it to the side of the hat to look like a feather or other decoration often worn there. The bottom shoe attached to the lower end of the rectangular body served as the waist and legs. There were two smaller pieces of metal welded onto the bottoms of the inverted horseshoe to make feet that actually held him upright. The "FrankenCowboy" metal, multipart body was spray-painted silver and his final touch was to cut a triangle piece of fabric from one of his red paisley handkerchiefs and tie it around his neck.

Axel and Kasi-Ann were perched together on the removed bench seat of the '76 highboy Ford Sam and Brett were restoring for his first pickup, watching Brett work and scratching on the three dogs who were thrilled to be inside by the glowing double-barrel stove. The oversized shop was not heated, but the stove would run you out of there by noon if it was started in the morning.

The bricks absorbed and retained the heat, making it a decent place to work as long as the double doors were shut.

An hour later, Brett glued the handle shaped out of deer antler onto the blade and put it in a vice to hold it until it dried. The sheath was already finished, so after the handle had dried, all that remained was to sharpen and polish the blade.

*****

The final days prior to the holiday were a blur. The first gift of the season appeared in the arrival of a letter from the mine declaring that Sam's number had been called and he would begin a position in Muck Haul in January. He passed his physical and all the other flaming hoops he was asked to jump through with flying colors and had nothing to do but wait for the days to tick by to the New Year.

The holiday season was always fast and furious, but by far Kat's favorite time of year. As they sat in the living room under the gentle twinkle of the Christmas lights on the tree and framing the window, Kat's cheeks shared the same rosy glow of happiness. She had worked during the day, effectively giving Sam the ability to work in the shop, scurrying to finish her gift in the nick of time, just the way he liked it. He thought about barring the door to the children just on principle when they followed him to the shop, but they ended up having a great afternoon hanging out together while he worked on the boot rack. The boys even had some helpful decorative ideas for the sides that Sam admittedly wouldn't have thought of himself.

They had attended the candlelight service, then returned home to do their Christmas Eve exchange of the homemade gifts.

## A Christmas Miracle?

Kat's was cleverly placed on the porch on their way out the door to church, so it was the first thing she saw when they returned, standing there with a giant red bow on it.

She was again awestruck at the amazing talents her family had. The tradition of making gifts instead of buying them was something she and Sam had started when the children were very young, trying to restore more of the reason for the season to the world's commercialized version of Christmas. They did provide one gift from Santa, encouraging their kids to think of one simple thing they really would like to have. The older they got, they could see that they looked forward more to the homemade gifts, both the ones they would make and the ones received, than the one that the would-be sleigh delivered.

Christmas morning also held the tradition of chocolate cake for breakfast. Nana Posie was born on Christmas day and adored warm chocolate cake with chilled fresh cream. Kat grew up celebrating the birth of the Savior and her mother together and happily passed it on to her own family, as her parents were usually there to spend the holiday with them. There isn't a kid in the world that wasn't thrilled with the idea of cake for breakfast, so the Christmas Day tradition lived on, despite its power to induce a sugar coma by noon. Sam, who had lived by the "Dessert First" rule his whole life, was of course, in complete support of the idea, regardless of the known disagreement he and his stomach would have over the issue later.

As if the holidays didn't present enough hustle and bustle with company and family parties and gatherings, church pageants and school concerts, Kat's birthday fell on New Year's Eve. She looked forward to it as not only her special day, but also the end to all of the holiday hullabaloo. It was nice to have such fun things to celebrate, but also wonderful to get back to what they considered their twisted sense of everyday normal.

The day after Christmas, or what Kat grew up knowing as Boxing Day, was traditionally known to be the world's biggest shopping day. All manner of gift exchanges and additional purchases were being made, as friends and family enjoyed their holiday vacations. The Patterson clan, however, would be sledding. Thermoses of coffee and hot chocolate were filled and numerous hats, gloves, coats, coveralls and the like were gathered up along regular sleds, 4-wheelers and the occasional snow mobile, when it was running. The three siblings looked like poster children for Carhart between bibs, coats and all the necessary gear for being comfortable outside in Montana winter weather.

They drove just north of the ranch right after breakfast to a favored hill on the property that was a prime sledding location. It was big enough that even the diehard kids preferred to have a lift going up after a couple runs, and the snowmobile was greatly appreciated when available. They started a bonfire off to the side of the base of the hill to cook hot dogs and s'mores over for lunch and to warm themselves throughout the day.

Each of the kids had their own sled. There was also a family sled Sam had fashioned out of an old satellite dish. He had resurfaced and painted the bottom and welded handles all the way around the edge so everyone could get a good hold. That proved to be a handy feature about the time he greased it with a layer of Pam cooking spray and sent it rocketing off the hill with just the kids on it that didn't weigh enough collectively to talk about.

They came screaming down off the hill at mock chicken and sailed across the trail at the bottom, careening into a massive bull pine. Axel had bailed off, rolling into the snowbank just before impact, leaving Brett to shelter Kasi-Ann. He instinctively rolled on top of her to shield her from hitting the tree, but she was still thoroughly unimpressed about being flattened by her older brother. She elected to stick to her own round, plastic, disk sled she dubbed Pink Lightning after that.

Kat, who was envisioning mass concussions, was furious, but more because Sam was laughing and cheering madly about how fast his creation would fly. He argued that he had indeed taken stock of their condition at the sudden end of their flight, and then, in error, might have again asked if she saw how fast that thing actually moved. It was decided that the family sled, should then only be used as that—as a family, with *everyone* on board.

The day was gloriously warm and sunny, making it a perfect sledding day. The undisturbed blanket of pristine, glistening snow had been positively begging to be baha'd through, and they had been beyond willing to oblige.

By the time the afternoon sun began to dip, they were all weary from both the fresh, frigid air and multiple trips up the hill. Ready to call it a day, they put out the fire, packed up and headed for home.

There was a strange car parked in the drive in front of the house as they idled back through the pasture towards the shop. Sam asked Kat if she knew who it was when he got back in after closing the gate behind them.

"No idea," she said, shaking her head.

An older woman in a long, white, wool coat stepped out of the car with Nebraska plates as they pulled up. Nobody recognized her. They figured she was lost and possibly looking for directions.

"I'll go see what's up if you guys will start packing stuff in the house," Sam offered.

He stepped out and walked toward her while everyone else gathered up the wet clothes and food items to take in.

"Hi, can I help you?" Sam asked, with his usual, warm, friendly smile.

"I hope so," she began somewhat timidly, and then went silent for a moment as she appeared to steady her composure. "I'm sorry, I've rehearsed this a thousand times in my head, but it is quite another business to be here in person. I don't really know how to say this, so I'll just get right to the point. I am here to talk to you about your mother."

Sam was instantly taken off guard and not entirely sure if it was meant to be some kind of joke or not, but there was nothing funny about it.

"Ma'am, I'm sorry, but my mother is deceased. She passed away several years ago," Sam said carefully, assuming she knew his mother, but was not aware that she had died.

"I know, dear, and I'm so sorry for your loss," she said with genuine sympathy. "In fact, I know that you tragically lost both of your parents, and while the timing would never be right, that's why I'm here." She took a deep breath, looking him squarely in the eye.

"*I* am your mother ... your *biological* mother."

# Sam and Kat

The playground bully only took five minutes to single out the new girl, never mind that there were only twenty-six students in the entire rural school elementary. Her bright-red, curly hair was just the first avenue of assault he chose, the small cascade of light-brown freckles across her nose and cheeks would undoubtedly be next, as the bloated toad of an assailant definitely did not look smart enough to conjure up his own material.

Kathryn Ann Heughan rolled her eyes at the continued insults from her idle swing. It was day one of the second grade in a little Montana town her father had chosen to buy a ranch near. They retained a lucrative farm in her old hometown, but this southwestern Montana, banana belt area promised a more favorable climate for raising cattle than their other one, barely two stones from Canada properties. The north wind and blizzard conditions there could leave them stranded on the place for weeks, barely able to get around, plowing out hourly with a tractor that was reluctant to start in the forty-below weather. The road cleared would simply blow back in with snow with nothing on the windswept, tree-devoid prairie to stop it. Her mother had also decided to come out of a semi-retirement and assist in the Title 1 teaching at school, making her existence in a new place all the more compromised.

"Well, aren't you going to say something, *Red?!*" the bully spat out.

*That's real original. Think of that all by yourself, did ya?* Kat thought to herself, trying to decide if this would merit a reaction of any kind, but in truth, the creep was tap dancing on her last second-grade nerve. She was no more afraid of his blustering than she was of any other storm that was more thunder than lightning. The kid was big, no doubt about it, but he was obviously slow and dimwitted. She also guessed he didn't know she had older brothers and was no stranger to a tussle. One well-placed, swift kick would knock all the air out of his foul mouth and lungs alike.

Kat glared up at the bully a few feet away, staying firmly planted in the swing, still contemplating her plan of action.

"I bet you didn't even go to a regular school where you came from. I bet your mom taught you at home, since she's the dumb kid teacher after all! What do you think, Jake?" he asked, dragging his obviously similarly dimwitted cohort into the conversation. "She looks like she's *home-teached* to me," he continued, making a deliberate error in wording to insinuate his opinion of her intelligence level.

*Oh, heck, nooo.* He could insult her all day long, but she would not keep her seat for someone running their mouth about her family. She bailed out of the swing and onto her feet.

"Oooh, I'm soooo scared," the bully jeered. "What are you going to do about it, runt?" he asked, sneering at her, looking her small frame up and down.

Kat opened her mouth to say exactly what she intended to do about it, but it was someone else's voice that came out.

"Knock it off, Jimmy!" a commanding voice sounded from directly behind her. Kat whirled around to see a lanky, sandy-haired boy standing there staring down the bully that now finally had a name, as if she cared. Mildly annoyed at the interruption of a situation she was obviously in full control of, she stood there looking at the newcomer with a cocked left eyebrow.

"Stay out of it, Patterson, it's none of your business," Jimmy retorted, but the now gathering group of students all noticed the two steps back he had already retreated. Her apparent rescuer was quick to advance, canceling out the distance with his own two larger steps.

"Problem here, Sam?" another new face inquired, butting through the student wall forming around the pair.

"Hey, Joe," Sam said calmly. "I was just asking Jimmy that same question. He seems to have forgotten his manners and should maybe try picking on someone his own size," Sam answered, still eyeballing Jimmy.

"Like *you?*" Jimmy blustered.

Sam's reply was simple. Jimmy didn't even see it coming, but Kat was way ahead of him. She saw Sam's right hand balled into a tight fist at his side as he advised him about picking on people. When Jimmy challenged him, his arm had moved like lightning. He single-stroked him right up under his jaw, simultaneously shutting his mouth and his lights off. He crumpled in a heap at Sam's feet.

"Well, okay," Joe said, looking at Sam in sheer amusement. This was clearly not abnormal behavior in his mind.

"Samuel! James!" Mrs. Barrett hollered from the step of the blue-and-white schoolhouse. The short, blonde, athletic PE teacher made her way to the now disbanding students. Jake had faded back into the group as they moved, but Sam, Joe and Kat stood riveted with Jimmy, now groaning in the dirt of the dual monkey bars and swing set combo.

"What the Hail Mary just happened here?" Mrs. Barrett demanded. "And Jonah, I'm warning you, I want a straight answer!" she thundered, addressing Joe by his full, proper name.

"Jimmy was giving the new girl a bad time, ma'am," Joe began, with a devil-may-care grin encompassing his face. "Sam just helped him see the error of his ways," he finished, biting his own lip, and clearing his throat to keep from laughing.

"Alright, you two, get him on his feet. *Now!*" she barked, gesturing at Jimmy who still hadn't made any attempt to get up. "We'll see if we can get to the bottom of this in the principal's office," she finished, her desire for them to follow her immediately evident.

Kat stood watching as Sam and Joe each got under an arm and hauled the still slightly incoherent Jimmy to his feet. They took off walking, dragging him along. For a scant second, Sam turned back and looked straight at her, smiled, and nodded, and then filed off to receive his sentencing.

CPSIA information can be obtained
at www.ICGtesting.com
Printed in the USA
LVHW011136270221
680113LV00012B/1030

9 781662 805783